Thirty – 1

The Complete Journey

By

Angelique LaFontaine

Printed in the United States of America

First Printing, 2022

ISBN 9798842297610

Angelique LaFontaine

7337 Havenridge Lane

Kaufman TX 75142

www.angeliqueartworkco.com

Thirty -1

The Complete Journey

By

Angelique LaFontaine

Reckless – Volume 1..Page 7

Salvation – Volume 2...Page 19

Boom – Volume 3...Page 31

The Therabs – Volume 4..Page 43

The Chimera Room – Volume 5.....................................Page 55

Premonition – Volume 6...Page 67

Theological Discussion – Volume 7.............................Page 81

The Social Control – Volume 8.....................................Page 93

Lines Have Been Drawn – Volume 9............................Page 107

Advanced Life Process Selection – Volume 10.................Page 121

PLEASE
DRIVE
SLOWLY

Ray woke up to the warm sun shining on his face through the white blinds that hung in the window. It was a summer morning in Los Angeles, California and he was starting his day the same as any other, slow moving and relaxed. The world was in pure chaos and he openly declared his complete and total separation from this chaos. Ray enjoyed and celebrated life and felt that everyone should be doing the same; unfortunately, that was just not the case.

The year was 1967 and the Vietnam conflict was of constant discussion. The country was separated down the middle. Families were torn apart and young men were being ripped from their home to fight in a "war" that nobody really knew too much about. Ray luckily was able to dodge the bullet of fate that was handed to so many others. He was never drafted into the war and felt that simply was because he was destined to help others understand that war, killing, and all-around violence was just not the direction that this world should be going.

At age 31, Ray still did not have much direction in his life. He did not have big dreams that involved him being a part of some huge corporation nor did he strive to be rich and famous. There was not much that he needed or wanted in the way of material things. He was a simple thinker in terms of just treat people well and they will treat you well. Enjoy your life while you are living it and you will be the happiest person around.

There was nothing spectacular in the way of looks for Ray. He stood at about 5 ft 8 inches tall. He was not overweight but had a look about him that suggested he was not athletic either. His arms and face and a slightly sun-tanned complexion. His dark brown hair was long and cascaded down his back. Often, you would see him with a bandana tied around his forehead. His face had a scruffy, unshaven look but his brown eyes were kind looking and even if he was not actually smiling, his eyes suggested that he was. All in all, he had a very pleasant looking and approachable appeal to him. Most people that he said hello to, often returned the greeting as his demeanor was contagious. Anyone that found themself spending more than 5 minutes with him, would say that they felt like better people around him. He was simply that pleasant.

He did not have any piercings, but he did have 2 tattoos on both sides of his neck. One tattoo was a lightning bolt and he got that because he was a huge Elvis fan and the lightning bolt was sort of the insignia for the team that worked with and for Elvis, it meant, "Done in a Flash." The other tattoo was one of a small rose. He got that one in remembrance of his mother. She had died when Ray was 16 years old. She had gotten sick, from what Ray still did not know. But she had died in his childhood home back in Iowa. When she died, Ray left town and never returned.

His father was never a part of his life and he was an only child, so he did not feel compelled to stay in Iowa. He wanted to experience things and go places. He wanted to meet as many people as he could. That was 15 years ago, and, in that time, Ray did exactly that. He lived the life of a wayward traveler. He never stayed in one place for too long but made many friends along the way. Some people that he would remember for the rest of his life and others that were only significant in the moment that he met them. All of them changed the course of his life in one way or another. And never did he part with people on bad terms.

Ray wasn't sure what happened when you died but also thought that the gamble of potentially running into those people again in this life or the next was too great of a risk, simply because people cling to their love and affection for an individual just as dearly as they do their hatred and vengeful thoughts.

Ray did not subscribe to religion, not that he thought it was a bad thing, but he just felt that the existence of an institution to simply teach people how to be good people was ridiculous. Ray thought that everyone had the ability to know the difference between right and wrong, regardless of their upbringing. All of the other "rules" that religion and churches had were established to do nothing more than develop a unified group of followers and in the end, amounted to nothing more than additional rules and guidelines to live by that were not your own. He found it extremely ironic that institution of religion was founded on the basis of giving people hope of higher being that was bigger than them and possessed an eternal love for all mankind but at the same time, it was the existence of this very institution that was the cause of almost all wars and the source of so much bloodshed throughout the world and has been for thousands of years.

Ray did not force his ideologies onto others but felt that it was his personal responsibility to live his life in a manner that supports what he campaigns for. Thus, Ray participated in many anti-war rallies, he supported any and all of his friends that were unlucky enough to be drafted but chose to flee their "civic" responsibilities; he also helped raise money to send more worthy individuals to Washington DC to help lobby congress and get change instilled from a legislative level. Ray was involved in a lot; he really was hopeful that the future was going to be a better place, one free of war and crime and a place that embraced peace and life. Although his ideas were considered by many as forward thinking and his lifestyle was looked at as lazy, and nonproductive, Ray did not care. He really believed that he stood for a greater good.

This morning though was going to introduce Ray to a situation that he could have never prepared for nor would he had ever dreamed was possible. Ray lived in an apartment with two other guys. It was a loft apartment so there were not closed off bedrooms, just one large living area. The guys basically crashed and slept wherever. It was not clean, and it barely had any furniture, just the way they liked it, free of the material items that aided in the corruption of others, masked by greed and envy.

"Wake and bake" was a normal way of life for these three. They would sit around and talk about their excursions from the night before. Some involved an act of anti-war vandalism or a protesting rally; some involved an intimate moment with a woman, and other stories involved a full-blown drink and smoke fest. Regardless of what happened the night before, these three guys were having the time of their life and really felt that they were the few that lived what they preached, no hypocrisy. Ray did not drink but he really enjoyed smoking his herbal therapy, otherwise known as weed. He did not recognize it as a drug simply because it was a plant that existed free and on its own in nature. It was not altered or tainted by the hands of man; besides, it helped him relax and identify more with the lifestyle he thought would promote a universal utopia.

After sitting around for a couple of hours, Ray decided that he needed to get out and do something, talk to people, just anything. He did not like the idea of being inside all day. His two roommates did not mind much; they would probably end up sitting around for the better part of the day until they decided what kind of party to go to that evening. Not Ray though, part of his life philosophy involved being a productive individual. He did not work a conventional job so the little bit of money that he earned was usually done so by the good graces of people he helped. Many times, as he walked around town, he would see people out in their yards doing work or building something, he would offer to help them. Sometimes he got paid and sometimes he did not. He did not focus on the monetary outcome but more the concept that the work he was doing was benefitting someone. That was far more fulfilling to him. He just could not understand why people got up every day to go to an office to do work that really, in the end, nobody really cared or noticed if it got done or not. How was that helping mankind?

Ray owned two pairs of jeans and three t-shirts; a blue tie-dyed shirt that a girlfriend made for him, grey t-shirt that simply had the name Nixon written across it encircled by a red circle with a giant 'X' going thru it, and a green shirt with a marijuana leaf on it. He did not need anything more; all three shirts encompassed the very essence of what he represented. Today, for sentimental reasons, he wore his blue tie-dyed shirt. He had not seen the girl that gave it to him in a long time but was sure that her birthday was coming up so in a way to him, he was commemorating it.

Ray said his goodbyes to his buddies, telling them that he would see them a little later; they were planning on meeting up at a party later, and left. He started walking down the sidewalk. The day was warm and bright. A lot of people were already out and about, running errands, going for walks and jogs, walking their dogs, whatever; this day was just too nice to be spent inside. Ray had fifty cents in his pocket, so his first stop was going to be at a coffee shop right around the corner from his apartment. He picked up his coffee to go and continued with this daily journey. Ray loved to walk; in fact, he did not even own a car. He loved the concept of using his feet and legs for the very purpose that they were intended, mobile transportation. Granted, he did not get places quick, but he was never in a rush to get anywhere.

It was about 11:45 in the morning on a Tuesday as Ray just walked and soaked up the beauty of the day. He was loving life and just taking in the scenery. He had been living in Los Angeles for about a year and even though he walked these streets every day, he looked at each person and shop as though he had never seen it before. The world was waiting to be discovered and embraced.

Ray sipped on his coffee as he walked down the narrow but busy street. The road turned and wound uphill and downhill until it passed all the shops that lined it and fed into an area that was lined with trees. It was a lot quieter and there were less people but the grassy surroundings on either side of him rolled into slightly rolling hills that made up a public park. People could be seen lying on the lush, green velvety grass where they daydreamed, read, wrote or just relaxed quietly. Ray stopped walking and stood on the sidewalk. He gazed out toward what seemed like an endless flow of greenery. He smiled at the simple beauty and mentally thanked himself for being wise and humble enough to enjoy such a view.

As Ray stood there, a slight cloud seemed to blow in and cover the sun. The slightly darker sky did not ruin the beauty of the day, rather what followed the permeability of the sunlight did. From behind, Ray heard a rumbling engine that seemed to grow louder and louder. He did not think anything of it as he was standing on a sidewalk and the road that ran next to it did have some regular traffic. However, something in Ray's stomach made him want to turn around. As he did, the rumbling of the car engine led into the screeching of tires brought about by a hard locking up of brakes. Ray, who was normally not very excitable, looked at the oncoming car wide eyed and panicked. He could not react fast enough to remove himself from danger, but he was aware of what was about to happen.

The car torpedoed itself toward Ray. The drunk but now panic-stricken driver fish tailed the car as the brakes tried to stop the car but failed miserably. Within less than 10 seconds, the car rocketed into Ray throwing him 25 feet into the air from the momentum of the out of control car. In that instant, all that could be seen was a coffee he was holding flying into the air like little rain pellets. Ray's shoes were knocked clean from his feet and Ray felt nothing. He did not feel any pain, but he certainly felt the jolt from the impact.

Ray's body hit the ground in one loud thud. His arms and legs bounced and then flopped to the ground in an unnatural position. Blood immediately started to flow from his head upon impact and his blue tie-dyed shirt turned dark red from an obviously deep laceration to his abdomen. He could hear people screaming around him and the sounds grew louder to suggest that they were running toward him, but he still felt nothing.

A quick blast of air blows across Ray's face and a loud snapping sound fills Ray's ears as his eyes flutter open. The last thing that he remembers was being hit by the car. Where was he now? He was lying on some type of bed but in an almost vertical, upright position. The bed was covered by a glass capsule that enclosed his entire body. Ray's arms and legs were in normal positions; nothing about them indicated that they could have been broken. He wiggled his toes and hands and then reached his right arm over to his left and pinched himself in the arm. He was not sure if it was real that if you pinch yourself while sleeping, you will awake but he figured it was worth a try.

The bed itself was not uncomfortable; in fact, it was soft and seemed to cater to the natural contours of the body. The sheets that lined the bed were white but as Ray ran his fingers over the fabric, could tell that they were not cotton. They felt weird, some sort of textured but woven fabric. It was obviously a synthetic material but what, Ray had no idea. There was no pillow nor cover blanket, just the bed.

As Ray's eyes began to focus, he looked around, first to his left and then to his right. All he saw from either direction were more people in the same type of encapsulated bed; all were looking around just as confused as he was.

The room everyone was in, or corridor as it appeared to be, had white shiny tile squares and the ceiling and walls were white too. It was very bright, but Ray could not tell what the source of the light was as he did not see any kind of fixtures. It looked like a hospital sort of setting but without doctors or nurses running around. In fact, there was not anybody walking around. Nobody came to check on the people as they awakened. Nobody was checking anybody's vitals or answering questions.

Ray wondered if it was possible that he survived the accident, but if he did, where was he and what was this place. The fact that he felt no pain but still had complete mobility of his body suggested to him that it was not quite as simple as surviving the accident. Unless, he had been unconscious for an extremely long time and this was some sort of weird rehabilitation center.

Looking down at himself, Ray noticed that he still had on the same jeans and blue tie-dyed shirt that he was wearing the day of the accident. But if he was in the accident, shouldn't there be tears or bloodstains or something? Nothing about this whole situation seemed normal and rational. Ray even questioned whether the accident even happened.

Maybe the whole thing was some type of weird hallucination brought about by too much sun and too much weed. Ray's thoughts were suddenly interrupted though.

As Ray thought these questions to himself, he heard a voice coming from above. It was a man's voice, deep and raspy but well-articulated. Ray looked around but could not figure out where the sound was coming from. It seemed to be all around him but coming from nowhere at the same time. Ray noticed that the other people around him were looking up too so he knew that whatever was going on, they would all be experiencing together.

"Hello everyone," the voiced bellowed throughout the corridor. "It seems as though everyone is slowly starting to awaken. I want everyone to remain calm. Each one of you is resting in an FX4 Cell. You are not going to be harmed but will be given an opportunity to understand what is going on. We will get started in a few moments so just take this time now to ensure that your eyes are functioning; if you feel so inclined, you can move your arms and legs as well. Please remember, now you have limited mobility."

Ray had no idea what an FX4 Cell was but knew that the bed he was lying in must be it. He looked around as much as he could. It was like being in a big glass coffin. There were hoses and lights flashing that seemed to react if he put his hand over them. He did not dare touch anything though. He had never seen anything like it before. Was he abducted by aliens? He remembers hearing about that whole Area 51 thing, and that was not too far away from Los Angeles. Maybe the whole thing with spaceships was real.

Ray could feel his heart rate increase. He felt alarmed and scared; none of this made any sense and his fear prompted him to become angry as he really wanted someone to explain to him what the hell was going on. After a few more moments, the bellowing voice returned, filling the endless room with its loud, mysterious voice.

The walls were bright white, and the air smelled of antiseptic. Lorraine walked down the hallway rolling her IV unit alongside her. She had been in the hospital for a few days now. About a year ago, she had been diagnosed with a terminal illness. At the time and due to the rapid decline in her health, the doctors gave her only a few weeks to live. The longevity that they gave her went from weeks, to months and now over a year. So really, nobody knew how long she was going to live. Because of the progressive decline in her health, Lorraine experienced other illnesses due to her body's inability to fight off infection. The doctors had no other choice than to just have her come in every month to treat these new illnesses as an attempt to at least make her remaining days as comfortable as possible.

Lorraine, whilst in the prime of her life, never fully understood the concept of Christian faith and what it truly meant to accept the Lord Jesus Christ as her savior. But being the mother of two children and the wife of a devoted husband, she found herself seeking out some type of explanation for her current situation. What she discovered was that there were no explanations for her situation. She had to find a way to accept that everything happens for a reason, that reason may not ever be known to her, but in the end, if she accepted the faith that Christians believed, she would also be able to accept the fact that her body dying was a part of a plan greater than her.

At 53 years old, Lorraine found that concept to be a great struggle, but she sought the help of a pastor in the hospital and spoke with him regularly while she stayed for her treatments. Together they prayed a lot and thru the Christian interpretation of the bible, Lorraine grew to be a very deeply devoted believer and came to terms with her situation.

Often, her husband would come and visit without the children and together they would pray for the strength to understand and trust in what was happening. Regardless of her acceptance, Lorraine couldn't get past the fact that she would very much miss her family and for that, she constantly prayed for the strength to enjoy the time that they had left together as opposed to wasting it on being angry and trying to find a reason why her time was going to be cut short.

The one thing that she held very dearly too in all of this was the reassurance from her pastor that she would in fact go to heaven. Since Lorraine had whole heartedly accepted Jesus and him dying for his love for mankind, she found a great deal of solace in knowing that she may be leaving behind her family but would soon be with her eternal family in heaven. It was this aspect that she held onto dearly and it was this comforting thought that she used to dry the eyes of her children as they wept when seeing their mother grow sicker and weaker.

This day Lorraine felt very weak and tired but as she walked past the windows in the hospital, she felt happy. The morning was clear and bright; there was not a cloud in the sky. It was 1967, in Des Moines Iowa. Lorraine was at the end of her stay in the hospital and was excited to go home to her family. She stopped walking to stare out the window. It was in mid-April so the air in the morning was cool and crisp and she longed to be outside and just breathe the air deeply into her lungs, and with any hope, even if just for a moment, could forget about the unfortunate demise that she was faced with.

Lorraine had always lived in Des Moines. Her parents had long since been deceased and she was an only child, so all her energy had been channeled into her own family. Lorraine never went to college, and she got married right out of high school, which in the 1960's in the Midwest, wasn't an uncommon thing. She and her husband had 2 children; Dotti was 13 and Joey was 15. Considering her age, they were younger than one would have expected. Lorraine and her husband struggled for years having children. They experienced miscarriage after miscarriage. The doctors could never figure out why her body kept killing the fetus, but Lorraine and her husband never gave up hope. They knew that if they just kept trying, that one day, their hopes would come true.

Lorraine walked away from the window as she continued down the hallway. Today was not going to be the day that she died; she knew that she would get to see her family again. Off to her right, was a wide stairwell that led to the main entrance of the hospital. It was the height of about 1 and a half stories and about 20 feet from side to side. She admired the grandiosity of the stairwell; for some reason, it always reminded her of grand central station. Not that she had ever been there, but the movies always depicted it as being a place of dramatic events. Long lost loves finding on another, rival gangsters having a shootout in old 1920's era; overall just a place of events taking occurring that etched their presence in the memory of others forever.

As she continued to walk, Lorraine caught a glimpse of herself in a mirror. She stopped and stared for a moment. She could no longer see the woman that she once was. Even though she was 53 years old, she looked more aged than that. Her once long blonde hair that flowed down her shoulders like golden silk now was silver and white. It no longer looked silky, it looked dry and tattered. Her soft, white skin was covered with wrinkles and seemed to hang from her body. Her incredible weight loss left her looking weak and frail. The one thing though that remained the same was the sparkle in her bright blue eyes. That sparkle radiated her longing for life and her love for her family. She clung to it and admired it.

She truly felt that her faith is what was keeping the life in her spirit and that spirit permeated the room with her beautiful blue eyes.

Lorraine turned away from the mirror and headed back to her room. The IV that was attached to her followed her around like a looming shadow that constantly reminded her that she was tethered to the reality of her mortal existence.

When Lorraine got back to her room, a nurse was waiting for her. The nurse smiled at Lorraine and asked how she was feeling today. Lorraine, always trying to remain pleasant, smiled at the nurse and just replied with, "Well, I woke up this morning so the day's already off to a good start."

Beth smiled saying, "That's my girl. You always know how to look at the positive, more people should have your outlook. They would probably enjoy life more."

Beth handed Lorraine two pills. The pills were some antibiotics to fight off a virus that was attacking Lorraine's kidneys. The infection itself was not fatal but rather just another reminder that Lorraine's body was not strong enough to fight it off itself. This kidney infection is the reason that Lorraine was hooked up to the IV in the first place. Her body was not retaining proper hydration, and with the kidney infection, she was subject to kidney failure. The doctors were confident though that the infection would pass. They were also hopeful that Lorraine's body would hold out long enough for them to discover the true source of what the problem was before she completely expired.

The antibiotics always made Lorraine sleepy. She felt relaxed about 15 minutes after taking them. Before the nurse left, she turned on the television for Lorraine and handed her a remote control that was cabled to the television so that she could change channels. Lorraine flipped through the channels and finally settled on a movie that she had loved since she was a child, "Gone with the Wind". Lorraine loved that movie and although she never agreed with Scarlet's behavior in the movie, she always found it admirable and courageous for an individual to have such conviction in her search for happiness. Granted, the people that she hurt and the way that she used them to discover what it was that would make her happy were not acceptable, but her desire to prove to herself that her existence wasn't an accident and there was someone or something that she was destined to be a part of. "It's all part of God's plan," Loraine mumbled to herself as she dozed off.

Lorraine was scheduled to be released the next day. So today, Lorraine was scheduled to receive an upped dosage of antibiotics before her release. Her next dosage was scheduled for 6 hours later, which would be around 3 in the afternoon; her final dosage would be at 9 in the evening. Before being released, the doctors would check her vitals and make sure that everything was stable enough for her to go home. Until then she would rest, hydrate and allow the medicine to work.

Lorraine vaguely remembered Beth coming in at lunchtime to bring her food. It all seemed like a dream. But when she woke up around 2 in the afternoon, she realized that it could not have been a dream. There was a covered plate on her table, an empty glass and a water pitcher on her table. She sat herself up in bed, completely famished; Lorraine lifted the lid of the covered plate. There was a sandwich, a fruit cup and some cheese cubes. Lorraine ate her meal in silence and drank two glasses of water; she waited another 15 minutes and drank two more glasses of water. She had heard someplace that if you drink your fluids while you eat, the fluids don't get properly absorbed into the body and so if you wait a bit after eating and then drink your fluids, it'll get absorbed better. Whether or not that was true, Lorraine had no idea, but she had done it for as long as she could remember.

After she finished her meal, Lorraine laid back down and flipped through the channels on the television. It was almost time for her 3 o'clock dose of medicine, so she just sat and waited. Like clockwork, Beth emerged into the room at 3 o'clock on the dot. Smiling, she handed Lorraine the two pills saying, "I'm glad you had an appetite. Shows that the medicine is working, and the infection must be close to gone if it is not already. Strong girl."

Lorraine smiled back and just said, "That's right, you won't see me just lie down and die."

The same as before, 15 minutes after taking the medication, Lorraine became very groggy and tired. She eventually dozed off. She did not know how long she was out for, but something abruptly woke her up. She sat straight up in bed and looked around. The surroundings she saw all seemed real but not real at the same time. All around her was white fog or something like it. She could not see the floor, the walls, or the ceiling. In fact, Lorraine did not even know if she was still in her room. She could see that she was still lying on the bed but curiosity got the better part of her and she hopped off, eager and afraid at what she would find beneath her bare foot as she stepped out onto where the floor used to be.

As soon as she got off the bed though, the white smoke engulfed the bed and within seconds, it was no longer visible. The floor or what used to be the floor did not feel like the cold tile that she was used to. It was solid but she could feel it travel up her leg and into her back, and yet, when she looked, there was nothing, just more smoke.

Off to her left, where the door used to be, the smoke appeared to part a pathway and there was a brightness that seemed to be glowing off in the distance. "Have I died?" she thought to herself. "I must be in heaven." At first, she felt exhilarated, she felt at peace. "There is a God, all of my faith was for the right things and I've finally come home," she thought to herself. Lorraine hastily made her way toward the path that had cleared away. She was positive that she was supposed to follow that path.

Lorraine walked with extreme caution as she proceeded onward. She could not see the floor and so she was not sure exactly where she was supposed to step. As she progressed forward, the path seemed to clear, giving her indication that it was okay for her to move on. Part of her apprehension and caution was that she really did not know what she was supposed to do once she found the end of the path. Would her lord and savior be waiting there for her with outstretched arms? Just like in the stained-glass windows she saw in church. Or would she find a group of others waiting for her. A group of believing souls that found their way just as she did; waiting for her to join them in eternal life.

Lorraine's feeling of happiness that she had found her salvation was quickly turned as she felt a weird sensation come over her. She had a feeling of falling, but her surroundings had not changed. An uneasy feeling in the pit of her stomach emerged and quickly swept over her body. Something did not feel right but she did not know what it was. She did not feel anything, no pain, nothing. But the feeling of falling and dread overwhelmed her.

A sudden jolt rocked her body and for a moment, she closed her eyes. When she opened them, she saw a light shining down on her. It caused her eyes to dilate and lose focus for a moment. She remained very still until she could see again. When her eyes were back to functioning properly again, she looked around. She became immediately alarmed with what she saw.

She saw that she was enclosed in glass capsule. She had never seen anything like it and the best way that she could describe it was like a big, glass coffin. There were lights flashing and tubes feeding in. Her immediate reaction was to start pounding on the glass, "Help!" she shrieked. "Beth! Please help me!" There was no reply.

Lorraine's vision ignored everything else around her as she scanned the room for any sign of movement. She was desperate to get somebody's attention. She did not care who. There was nobody.

Realizing that her legs were not bound to anything, Lorraine immediately started kick the glass. Her efforts were useless. Her kicks did not leave behind a crack, a dent, not even a scratch. Lorraine panicked more. She started screaming frantically and pounding on the glass. Her hair flung from side to side and stuck to her face from the perspiration that was collecting on her.

Amidst her screams, she heard a distinct hiss sound. She could not tell where the sound was coming from, but the capsule began filling with a very fragrant smell. The smell calmed her and for a second, she was distracted by it. She closed her eyes and inhaled deeply. "Lavender," she thought to herself. She smiled as she continued to breathe in the perfumed air. She remembered loving that smell as a child. As a child she had always been fond of that smell. It reminded her of springtime and being outside amongst the flowers and playing with her friend. The more her mind drifted down memory lane, the calmer she became. She thought of being a child, she thought of home and for some reason, felt incredibly safe.

Lorraine continued to baste in the serenity that was being cultivated in her mind by the lovely smell that filled her capsule. She opened her eyes and looked around. She felt very calm and relaxed. She looked around outside of the capsule and noticed other capsules lining the walls of the long corridor she found herself in. She wondered where she was. She never recalled ever being in this room in the hospital before. She tried to recall what happened right before she had found herself in this little glass coffin, but could only recall be seeing the white, billowy smoke. She did not know if that was a dream or if this was a dream. She knew that she had to still be in the hospital though. She could not have been any place else.

A smile crept across her face as she once again enjoyed the tranquil aroma that was filling her nostrils. Once again, she closed her eyes and inhaled deeply. When she opened them, she noticed all kinds of strange looking lights inside the capsule. They were blinking in sporadic manners. There were tubes feeding in and out of the capsule. She had never seen anything like it and could not even begin to describe what she was seeing.

When she looked out of the capsule again, she noticed lights coming from the ceiling but could not find the source. "How strange," she thought to herself. "There were lights, but no fixtures?" She became even more confused. She did not understand how that could even be possible.

Her observations were unexpectedly interrupted though. A voice became audible, but Lorraine could not tell where it came from. It was all around her, yet she could not find the source. "Greetings everyone, I see that you are all awaking…"

Boom – Volume 3

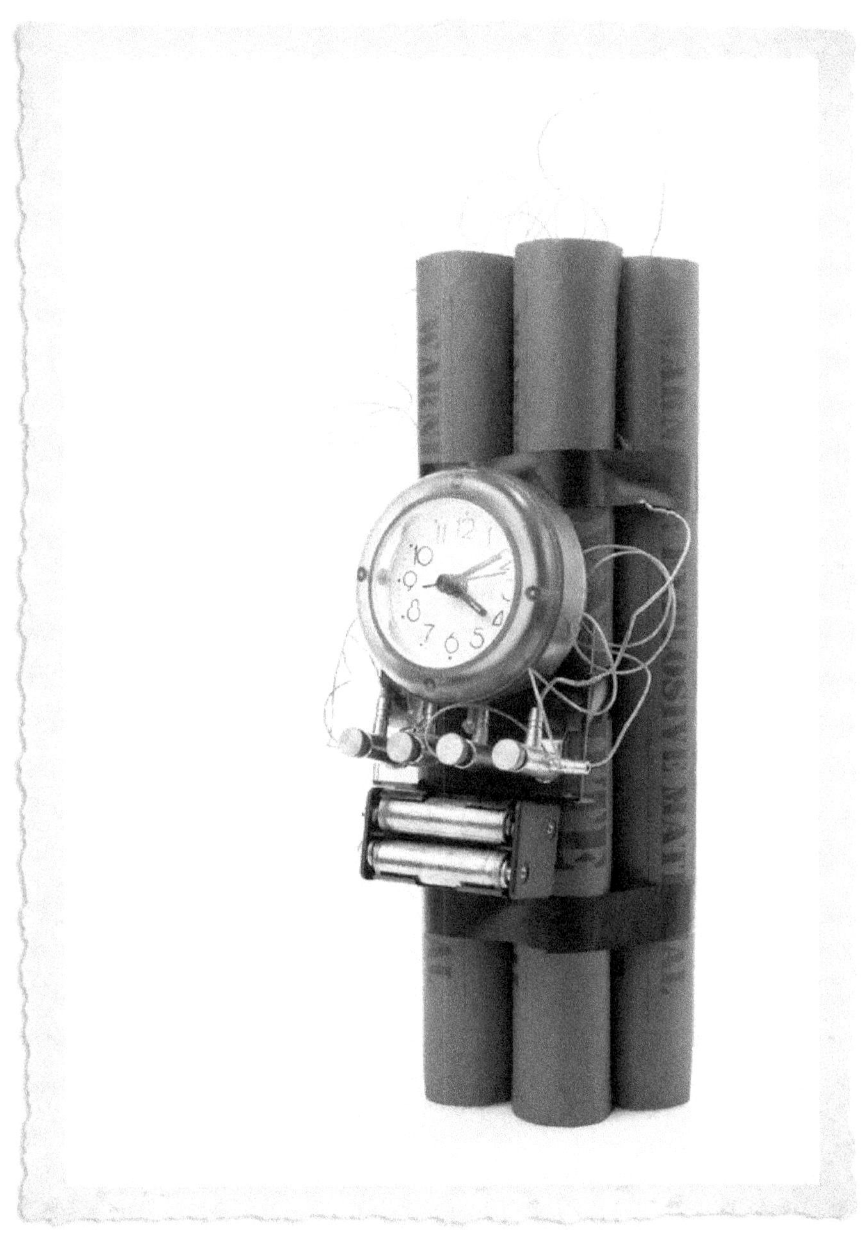

The doctor was standing in the middle of the examination room when they rolled the gurney in. On the gurney was a black body bag that took up the length of the gurney. The orderlies rolled the gurney to the center of the room and unzipped the black bag revealing a lifeless body. An older woman lay inside the black bag. Her skin looked like a grayish clay kind of material. She lay there dead as the doctor looked over her lifeless corpse. He read the tag that had been attached to her foot, and he read out loud, "Lorraine Caster."

The doctor put on some rubber gloves and began the examination. The orderlies handed the doctor a chart and quietly walked out.

The examination room was dark and morbid. All that could be seen were medical tools that were obviously used for postmortem purposes. Partially dissected human bodies lined the walls of the room. The room smelled of death and the dim lighting that shown down only added to the morbid ambiance that filled the air.

Dr. John Anderson was a medical researcher at a research hospital in Bridgeport, Connecticut. He was a medical researcher for the University of Connecticut but worked out of the hospital in Bridgeport. He had been doing research for many years and specialized in virus and bacterial infections. Most of his research was based off the body's reaction and ability to fight off disease. Dr. Anderson was both accredited and chastised for his forward thinking in the field of medical research

It was 1967 and Thomas Starzi had performed the world's first successful liver transplant. Dr. Anderson followed a lot of the work of Starzi and was a great admirer of him. Conservative thinking paved the way for medical bureaucracies that limited the type of research that Dr. Anderson could do. Nonetheless, Dr. Anderson upheld his beliefs of one day being able to utilize the advancements of medical technology; he upheld those beliefs with great dignity. He envisioned a way for the medical industry to one day be able to utilize existing tissues or cells to be able to find a cure for medical ailments that people suffered from. He often wondered if there was a way for mankind to produce and cultivate their own tissues or cells. For now, though, he was limited to researching expired tissues of the deceased and find out as much as he could in doing so.

Dr. Anderson's assistant came into the examination room holding a notepad and a pen.

"All right let's see what we've got," the doctor said as he lifted his face mask into place.

"Caucasian woman, age 53. She had been diagnosed with a terminal disease that appeared to attack her immune system primarily, however, was constantly suffering from other ailments and afflictions brought on by this disease," Doctor Anderson read from the chart. "Actual cause of death was cerebral hemorrhaging in the left, back membrane." He looked at the dead woman's shaved head and saw the fracture skull.

The assistant, Mark, was taking notes the entire time. "How did that happen? Can you tell?"

"Well, from what I understand, she fell down a flight of stairs or something. I was not given a lot of specifics. She is a donor, so a lot of immaterial information is withheld. It's an act of sensitivity to the family," the doctor explained.

Dr. Anderson and Mark continued with their examination for another couple of hours. They took multiple measurements and removed some tissue from numerous places of the woman's body. Before calling it a night, the doctor draped a white cloth that almost glowed under the dim lighting in the examination room. He and Mark bid each other a good evening then left.

Dr. Anderson lived only a few blocks away from the hospital, so he walked to and from work. This evening, it was a little chilly, but he did not mind. It was a little after 9 pm and was already dark out, but again, he did not mind. The pavement was slightly wet from the moisture that was accumulating. The fragrance of the wet, freshly mowed lawn filled the air. It was indeed a tranquil evening. Dr. Anderson liked the cool night air. He found it refreshing after spending so many hours in the dank bowels of the hospital with all those corpses. He felt rejuvenated after his walk; he felt as though he could continue walking for hours and never grow tired of the relaxing, calming feeling that engulfed his body. This evening though, that was a good thing. The calmness and tranquility was what he was going to need this evening; he had a lot of work to do.

Dr. Anderson lived in a small apartment by himself. His wife had long ago died and his children, he only had 2, lived out on the West Coast and did not stop to visit nor call very often. Both were adults with their own families; Sara, who was 28 years old and Justin who was 33 years old. He had not seen either of his children in probably 5 years. There was not a huge quarrel or falling out between any of them; they just stopped coming around when the chaos of normal life consumed them. He never faulted them but always thought that if they put forth a little effort, or even invited him to visit them, the relationship would not have become estranged. Whenever he gave it a slight thought, he did feel a bit of despair come of over him as he never even met his grandbabies. He never really understood why either. To compensate though, he just kept himself busy and occupied. Despite that though, Dr. Anderson's life was quiet and small, and he liked it.

When he walked into his apartment, he was greeted with darkness. He flipped the light switch on revealing a quaint but tidy little haven. There was a small kitchen table with 2 chairs in his kitchen/eatery area. He had a lazy boy recliner and a television set in the living room. His bedroom had a small twin size bed and matching dresser bureau. On his bureau, he kept a photograph of his wife and a shoe polishing brush and its polish. The entire apartment smelled of pipe tobacco. Not the kind that left a bitter taste in your mouth after breathing it, but the sweet kind, the kind that when you closed your eyes, you would automatically think of Sunday afternoons, and gracious old men reading the newspapers while smoking on their pipe. The kind of old men whose eyes twinkled with kindness and they seemed to wink at everyone in a way that suggested that they knew something that the others did not.

Across from the bedroom was a small study. This is the room where Dr. Anderson spent most of his time. In it, were blueprints, physics books, chemistry books and multiple different canisters marked with odd names that to most be unfamiliar. The only familiar phrase on all the canisters was the word EXPLOSIVE.

Dr. Anderson sat down at his desk and rolled up his sleeves. He reached inside of his desk drawer and pulled out a notebook. He began reading the entries that he had made from some of the previous nights. Occasionally, he would sit and stare at his formulas and calculations and in a frustrated effort, reference the textbooks and reference books he had by his side to verify what he had written was correct.

After sitting there for about an hour, he heard his stomach growl. Putting down his notebook and pencil, Dr. Anderson walked into the kitchen and made himself a sandwich. He stood over the kitchen sink while he quietly ate and continued to think about the information he had just gone over. When he took the last bite of his sandwich, he clapped his hands together over the sink to shake loose any crumbs. From there, he went back into his office.

Dr. Anderson glanced over his notes one last time and then walked over to a small work bench that he had set up in his office. He carried 3 of the canisters with him and set them very carefully on the work bench making sure that they were not touching one another. He then went to a small shelf where he had numerous beakers and petri dishes stacked up. He grabbed a few and placed them on the work bench as well. Finally, he grabbed a set of blueprints that had all kinds of formulas and measurements written on them. As well, there was a rough hand drawn sketch of an odd looking capsule looking device. It had propellers drawn on it and a small motor sketched out on it. There were rough measurements dimensioning out this device too.

He set the blueprints down next to the canisters. He lifted the lids off the canisters in a very gingerly fashion and set each one down next to its appropriate canister, making sure not to mix any of the lids up with the wrong canister.

Dr. Anderson grabbed a measuring spoon and confirmed the portion of the first substance he was about to scoop. Upon doing so, he held his breath and dipped the measuring spoon into the first substance. It was a white powder, odorless and with no significant visual attributes.

The moment that he lifted the measuring spoon out of the canister, Dr. Anderson heard a squealing of tires, a honking of horns and then a loud thud. The noise startled him, breaking his concentration. His hand waivered and the contents of the measuring spoon fell directly into the open, neighboring canister. There was a flash, and before he could realize what had just happened, there was nothing.

The residents of the surrounding houses of the small 4-unit apartment building that Dr. Anderson lived in; saw nothing more than a huge flash coming from the small upstairs apartment unit. A few seconds later, the flash was followed up with a series of explosions that wiped out the entire apartment building. The windows were blown out of the neighboring houses along with various external structural damages. Nobody knew what had just happened, but everyone cautiously made their way outside to see what was going on.

The fire truck sirens could be heard within minutes and all that was left of the tidy little, quaint apartment that Dr. Anderson lived in, were remnants of a building structure. There were no survivors, nor remains that could offer any type of explanation to what had just happened.

Dr. Anderson opened his eyes and looked around. He was very calm as he did so. His nature was to collect facts and data before drawing his hypothesis. So that is exactly what he did. He noticed that he was on some type of a bed, but he was not lying down. He was in a vertical, upright position but slightly slanted. He was not tied down, so his hands and legs were free to move. He ran his fingers over the surface of the bed that he was on. The texture was not cotton or polyester to his knowledge. It was something else, but he did not know what. He noticed that he was in some type of a case. He reached out and touched the surface. It was transparent but was not glass. He could tell that it was some type of plastic, perhaps a polymer he was unfamiliar with. There were lights blinking in no fashion. There were tubes feeding into the enclosure that he was in as well. He held his hand out in front of the tubes to see if he could feel any type of gas, air, anything being fed in. He felt nothing. What he did notice though was that his hands, once old, covered in wrinkles and liver spots, no longer were. They looked youthful. He touched his face. The once bearded, old face that he wore as a result of aging, felt cleanly shaven. The skin felt tight and taunt. "Am I even alive anymore?" He thought to himself.

Dr. Anderson looked outside of the capsule that he was in. He noticed immediately that he was one of many in a long corridor that was lined with many other capsules. Each capsule, he could see, had others in them. He could see the other people looking around, confused and frightened. Some of the people were pounding on the odd glass in a frantic way but would suddenly stop. They were not being killed but something was happening to them to calm them down and fast.

Dr. Anderson looked up and saw a series of lights positioned in the center of the ceiling. They went the length of the ceiling in both right and left directions. What he found most intriguing was that he could see the lights but could not find a source. Dr. Anderson squinted his eyes in hopes that they could refocus without the pupil dilation brought about from the bright glare of these luminescent spectacles, but he had no such luck. There was no light source that he could see.

A voice came out of nowhere and could be heard everywhere, but again, Dr. Anderson could not find the source of the sound. "Greetings everyone. I see you are all waking up. When everyone is awake, we will get started, so please just wait patiently." Dr. Anderson, more of the reactionary, did exactly that. He waited.

He continued to look around as he waited. He was not sure what he was waiting for but was very much intrigued. About 5 minutes passed and there was an odd buzzing sound that filled his capsule. The glass lifted and then slid to the side of the capsule. Everyone else's capsules did the same.

The voice came back and spoke again, "Please everyone, feel free to exit your FX4 cells. Walk around for a few minutes and get reacquainted with your bodies."

Dr. Anderson did just that. He stepped out of his capsule, or what was referred to as his FX4 Cell, and took a few steps. Others around him did the same. In normal human reaction, everyone immediately started to ask one another what was going on. Nobody had any answers. Dr. Anderson, however, did not speak to anyone. He just observed. He took a mental note of what it was that he was doing right up until he found himself in this place. He remembered the accident that happened right outside his home that startled him and caused him to mix up the chemicals, but that was it.

The voice came back on and announced, "Okay everyone, if you will look down on the floor, you will notice that there are white tiles, I am going to light up every other tile and I want everyone to stand in a tile that is lit. Believe me, there is no reason to be alarmed, this is to simply organize everyone in rows so that we can get everyone split into smaller groups."

Dr. Anderson looked down and saw a tile light up. He immediately stepped onto it and waited. The initial chaos that had infiltrated the room was subsiding and the other people were following the instruction as well.

After a few moments, everyone had found a tile to stand in and were all facing forward, or what they thought was forward.

The voice came back on and started to speak again, "Hello everyone, first and foremost, I want to welcome you all back. You have had a long journey and I know that you have a lot of questions. I am going to give you some of the basic information and then you will be split up into smaller groups to handle more intimate questions or concerns that you may have. If you have not already noticed, you will now. You are all younger than you remember. Each one of you died in the year 1967, however, you are all now at the age of 31 and the year is now 4883. Please do not be alarmed as you are all a part of a remarkable process that has been developed and implemented. Please get acquainted with your surroundings when the time is appropriate. I want to personally welcome some of our celebrity arrivals here today. Among us is the famous Jack Ruby, whom we all remember as the man who killed Lee Harvey Oswald, the assassinator of the great John F. Kennedy, we also have the great Robert J Oppenheimer who was the creator of the atom bomb. And of course, my personal favorite, Otis Redding who, if we are lucky enough, could perform for us all at one point."

As the voice said this, the crowd began to look around trying to find some of these celebrity individuals just mentioned. The corridor was filled with a sea of people and so it was almost impossible to know where to look. As well, everyone was instructed to remain on their tile and because this mysterious voice, although sounding human but undetectable, was bearing no immediate threat to anyone.

"I am extremely excited to be working with this group of individuals. All of you were a part of a particularly important decade and I absolutely cannot wait to have some conversations with some of you. The 1960's were a personal favorite of mine," the voice continued. "Now, I am going to excuse myself for a little while and everyone will be grouped together into smaller sections. Please look down and your tile will change colors, join your group that shares in the same color tile as you," the voice completed its statement.

There was a short pause and then the intercom came back on, only this time, instead of a voice, it was playing music, "Sit-ting by the dock of bay…"

The Therabs — Volume 4

The room was filled with a low murmur of voices as everyone gradually started to organize themselves as instructed. There was an electronic humming sound that filled the air, and the rows of FX4 cells that lined the walls of the room began to recess into the walls. Once the cells were flush with the walls, a white partition lowered from the ceiling and sealed the cells behind it.

The tiles that were lit up immediately became occupied with individuals standing on them. The voice came back on and made another announcement saying, "Thank you everyone for being so patient. Once again, please find a lit-up tile to stand on. There is no specific tile that you need to look for; just please go ahead and find one. In a few minutes I am going to change the color of the tile to a specific color; it will be either green or blue. Once you notice the color of your tile, please join the rest of the individuals that have the same color. Once you have done so, I will section you off again and then again. The point of this is to get all of you into smaller groups. Each group will be assigned an instructor for further explanation. Again, thank you for your patience."

Within minutes, the room began to split. At first, the blue and green tiles split the people up into two groups, then the tiles lit up with red and yellow colors, sectioning off everyone even further. Yet again, the tiles then lit up to orange and brown colors. The groups became smaller and smaller and the room that was once filled with what appeared to be hundreds of people scattered about and looked to have more order and method.

The groups dispersed into clusters of about 6-8 people. Ray and Dr. Anderson were standing side by side. They acknowledged each other with a nod but were far too curious to notice anything else. Lorraine was in the same group but less coherent as Ray and Dr. Anderson, as she was still subdued by the aromatic fragrance of lavender that had sedated her while she was in her cell. Dr. Anderson stared at Lorraine for a moment; he knew he knew her but just could not quite place her. Another individual that he took special notice of was Robert J Oppenheimer who was the creator of the atom bomb. Dr. Anderson was quite intrigued that this particular individual was in his group and vowed to make a special effort to get to know this man a little better, as to Dr. Anderson it would appear that they had similar interests.

After a few more minutes of just standing around and waiting, men came out from some doorway that had gone unnoticed before and they walked down the center of the corridor. They were dressed all in white and looked like orderlies. One at a time, each man stopped next to a group and began talking. The man that stopped next to the group that Ray, Lorraine and Dr. Anderson was in, began to speak.

"My name is Matthew; I will be delivering your orientation and providing you with a guide for today. I want to first welcome you all. What I want to do first is to bring you up to speed on what exactly is going on as I am sure that you are all very curious. I would ask though that you save all questions for after I have completed this introduction. Afterwards, I will give you a tour of this facility and the exterior grounds; then we will get something to eat."

Ray looked around and could tell that all the other orderly looking men were giving each group a similar speech. As Matthew began to speak more though, Ray was easily able to drown out the noises from the other groups until the only sound his ears picked up was the voice of Matthew.

Lorraine had a very worried look on her face the more that Matthew spoke. It was obvious that the sedative that she had been given was beginning to wear off. She did not say anything but looked like a scared rabbit that, even with the slightest sound, could take off at any moment and scamper away as though her life depended on it.

Dr. Anderson listened intently to what Matthew was saying but kept an eye on Mr. Oppenheimer the entire time. He studied the man's mannerisms and watched his facial expressions. Dr. Anderson could immediately tell which pieces of information interested the man and which pieces of information did not. "Body and facial expression give away so much," Dr. Anderson thought to himself. Dr. Anderson had always been pleased with his skills of observation; he knew he had a knack for it and was going to capitalize on that skill as much as he could.

Matthew continued to speak while the 3 individuals had their own private thoughts. "Okay everyone, as was previously stated, the year is 4883. Each and everyone one of you had in fact died. What you all commonly share is the fact that each of you died in the year 1967. In the last, 2900 years, there have been significant advancements in technology, medical research, and habitation accommodations," Matthew paced slowly in front of the group as he spoke.

"The facility that you currently find yourself in is called ALPS, which stands for the Advanced Life Process Selection. What we have been able to do is bring our deceased back to life. Through many, many years of research and endless trials and errors, the technique of taking dead tissue and giving it life, has been completed and perfected. The concept itself has much to do with harnessing energy that naturally exists. You can think of our bodies as a giant circuit and all we needed to do was find the capacitors that existed within it. These capacitors act as the storage devise for the energy and if you understand the concept of energy not being created nor destroyed, then it should come as no surprise to you that even though the body may have expired, the "capacitors" that our bodies have, had never been discharged. Now the interesting thing, which was discovered, and this took a lot of work to fine tune, because the body is organically based, it of course began the decomposition process immediately upon death. However, you can never mistake the fact that the human body is a remarkable thing that can naturally regenerate itself. This proved correct when shortly after we discovered a way to release the energy from the body's capacitors, the body did exactly what it was designed to do, it began to rebuild itself. Some of you were in very rough shape so, of course during your regeneration process, we had to help you out a little."

Lorraine did not wait for Matthew to finish speaking. She immediately shrieked, "I was dead?! And you brought me back to life?! Is this some kind of sick joke? This isn't funny!"

"Now ma'am," Matthew began, "I know that this is hard to believe but you're going to have to wait until I am done explaining everything. I'm sure that it will all make sense once I've done so."

This silenced Lorraine enough to listen a little bit more to what seemed like absolute ridiculousness.

"To continue on," Matthew started again, "Once the reactivation of human tissue had been completed, years and years of research was spent on determining the age that an individual should be brought back as. Since we as the technology and medical personnel had that decision to make, we needed to make sure that in general, it would be suitable for more than 80% of the populous that was brought back. The ages that we chose and tested on ranged from 18 to 45. The age that we settled on was 31."

Everyone just looked around at one another then began to study themselves a little closer. They felt their faces, touched their hair, looked at their arms and some of the older people who hadn't been agile in quite some time, began to move their legs and bend their knees free of pain and discomfort.

"Can I please still have your attention?" Matthew said to everyone, holding his arms up in the air to get everyone's attention. "Please, let us continue on. The reason that the age of 31 was chosen was simply because we found that age 31 is the most productive, the healthiest and the body is in its prime for regeneration. You will live a normal life and will not experience any kinds of disadvantages since you have been brought back. It is important for you to recognize and understand though the fact that you will 1, never get any older than 31 and you will never die. And 2, you are still a part of the human race, but you are now referred to as the Therab Race. This is not a secondary race as we do not recognize a class system like that. But your needs are going to be slightly different from the Plerab Race, the Plerabs are the ones that have not undergone the regeneration process yet, but they will. Everyone does.

It is important for you to know that you are currently living on Earth; however, the human race does in fact populate the rest of the planetary system as well as multiple galactic cities that have been tethered off of some of the planets and simply orbit. You will be given brochures later and we will explain the differences between each system and the benefits that each one has."

"So, if I am understanding you correctly," Ray began, "You are saying that we were all brought back to life almost 3000 years after our death at age 31. People are living out in space and we will never die?"

"In short," Matthew said, "Yes, that's the general gist of it."

There were a few snickers in the crowd, but nobody out right said that they did not believe anything that they were hearing.

Matthew could sense the skepticism and assured everyone saying, "I know that this is all impossible to believe but if you will all just bear with me for a little while longer, you will see that this is in fact real. Now I am going to ask all of you to form a single file line and follow me. I am going to show you around the facility and then we will go to the exterior grounds."

Matthew began walking and the group followed him. They approached the wall of the corridor that they were in and immediately a door, similar looking to an elevator door slid open. As the group walked, Matthew went on to explain to everyone the different facets of the ALPS facility. There were harvesting rooms where bodies were kept until they had reached full regeneration, there was what they called the legacy room where people spent hours upon hours tracking down the family members the people that were being brought back, and there was a monitoring room where workers sat in front of huge, transparent screens that displayed real life images of the activities going on in and around the ALPS facility.

The more information that everyone was given; the more that this whole thing seemed like a reality. The members in the group, for the most part, did not start to panic but they did start to take inventory of the questions that they felt were important to ask. However, being humbled into realizing that they had no idea where they were, what they were, nor what to expect when they left the facility, everyone continued to remain quiet until the end of the tour.

Matthew continued to lead the group on their parade of information. He led them to a huge room that looked like a bubble and was mainly constructed of glass. The group just looked outside in complete awe-struck fascination. There was not a cloud in the sky; the grass was impossibly green, and it looked so bright and clean. Almost like a painter had painted this huge, perfect image of how the world should look and wrapped it around the planet like an eggshell.

Two doors that slid open like elevator doors opened and allowed the group to go outside. Matthew smiled as he saw the expressions of everyone, "These are the exterior grounds everyone. They are a part of the ALPS facility but are open for usage of everyone.

The group dissipated a little but did not wander off from one another. The air was clean and crisp at a perfect 83 degrees. The sun gave off the perfect amount of radiation that seemed to just kiss your skin and then bounce off. There were unique plants everywhere. None of which were species that anybody had seen before. The colors were vibrant but, some of the plants looked as though 2 different kinds had been chopped into 2 sections and then mated together. Roses were growing on trees, bushes and shrubs were bearing fruit like apples and peaches. It was shocking to see but beautiful at the same time.

Ray could not help but walk up to the trees and the plants and touch them. He wanted to know what they felt like. Dr. Anderson studied very closely the texture of the grass. He understood the concept of cross pollination between plants but had never seen it invoked to this extent.

A shadow that cast itself overhead quickly diverted his attention away from the plants though. Dr. Anderson quickly looked up and saw what he thought was one of the most amazing things ever and could not believe that he did not see it before. Machines that looked like cars floated through the sky. They did not make a sound nor give off fumes; they just floated like apparitions and glided seamlessly. People were inside these machines. It did not look like they were operating anything, just sitting there as passengers. He then noticed the buildings. Some of them were on the ground and others floated freely in the air. They were all around him; it was a miraculous sight, but he pinched himself quickly because it all seemed like a vivid yet extremely unusual dream. It was in that instant that Dr. Anderson realized that he did not hear any noises at all. Nothing industrial that is. All he heard were birds and the low murmurs of the voices from people around. That shocked him. There were no motors, or generators. There were no power lines or smokestacks; nothing. Dr. Anderson just stood in place and stared at everything. He was trying so hard to fathom what he was seeing but this was beyond even his comprehension.

Lorraine was having a harder time taking everything in stride like the others. She too saw the hybrid plant life, the flying cars and the floating buildings. She also noticed bizarre looking animals and became greatly alarmed when she saw that they were roaming free; carnivores by nature, but none the less, strange looking. Tigers with hooves and jaguars that were the size of horses roamed around the grounds. She watched the animals intently and stood still frozen in fear. But never once did the animals advance on her or anybody else. They just walked around and grazed. Some were sunbathing in the middle of the open fields while some lounged from tree limbs.

The reality of what she was seeing enraged her. "This was all really happening," she thought to herself. Lorraine quickly walked up to Matthew and tapped him on the shoulder to get his attention. "You weren't lying, and you didn't drug us?"

Matthew just looked at Lorraine, he was not sure what her fury was being derived from, so he let her continue.

"I died! I was supposed to go to Heaven! You took that away from me. Who do you people think you are? How dare you make this decision for us! I am a Christian and I do not believe in this. I had prepared my soul, but not for this!" Lorraine was screaming at Matthew now.

In a calming and soothing voice, Matthew put a hand on Lorraine's shoulder and softly said, "Lorraine, there is no Heaven. In almost 3000 years of research, we would have been able to prove its existence. And if there was even the slightest possibility of the fact that it existed, these advancements and endeavors would never had been pursued. There is no salvation, or spirit world, Heaven or Hell. There is only death. I know that comes as a shock because the entire structure of your belief system is based on a blind faith. But please trust me when I say this; we have found a better way for mankind to exist and flourish, and we know that once the shock of all of this wears off, you will very quickly embrace and be grateful for the opportunities that await you around each and every corner.

There was sincerity behind what Matthew was saying and Lorraine's rage quickly turned to sorrow. "But what about my family? I thought that I would see them again."

Matthew smiled softly and said, "You will." He then turned his attention to everyone in the group and motioned for them all to gather around him. "Ok everyone, for the next 30 days you will be residents of the ALPS facility. You will be given 1 on 1 sessions with a doctor that will work with you on an individual basis." Matthew looked at Lorraine directly when he spoke next, "Your family has already been contacted and you will be given the opportunity to meet each and everyone one tomorrow. They will be introduced via generation, starting with the generation that was living in and around the time that you initially perished. Now we are all going to go back inside and get some food. From there, you will be given maps of the facility and of the grounds, then you will be shown to your sleeping quarters. So, if you all will follow me back inside."

Ray, Lorraine and Dr. Anderson stood shoulder to shoulder as they were facing Matthew while he gave his instructions. All three diverted their attention to the ALPS facility. The building was endless; it pierced the sky without an end in sight. It seemed to go on forever. People could be seen walking around inside and the silent machines that floated through the air hovered around the enormous building. It was an entirely new world that they were a part of.

The Chimera Room – Volume 5

Ray, Lorraine and Dr. Anderson all walked back into the ALPS facility together. They stood in what looked like the main lobby of the building. Matthew walked in behind them and addressed the group one more time. "Ok everyone, we are going to break for about an hour or so. Each of you will be escorted to your room. In there, you will find a map of the building, schedules and times for events and lectures that will take place and an instructional manual for your day to day needs. I urge you all to take advantage of everything made available to you. This life is going be quite different than your previous one and the intent behind everything we offer here is to make your transition painless and seamless."

As Matthew finished up his speech, a white door slid open. It looked to be a part of the wall that was to the left of the group; until it opened, nobody knew it was there. It made way to a long hallway that was brightly lit, and it too was the same, bright, sterile white color as everything else.

Motioning toward the hallway, Matthew finished addressing everyone, "Please go ahead and make yourselves comfortable. Feel free to walk around as much as you would like. Your names are printed on the door of the room you have been assigned to. To enter, run the palm of your right hand across the name plate on the door. Make sure that your hand touches the name plate, your ID is established by a cross reference against your palm print and your DNA. You will not be able to gain access to your room or any other room in the facility if a match is not established. I will make an announcement but let us all try to meet back here in an hour for lunch."

Ray, Lorraine and Dr. Anderson cautiously approached the hallway. In a single file line, they walked down the corridor; it looked like it went on forever. On both the right and the left side were doors; one about every 7-8 feet. There were nameplates on each door just as Matthew said that there would be.

After passing a few doors, the group noticed that the names were in alphabetical order followed by the birthday. Dr. Anderson was the first to find his name, running his hand across the name plate; he appeared to be enjoying this new little adventure that he was on. His door slid open and he immediately, without hesitation, slipped inside. He did not say anything to Ray nor Lorraine as his door closed behind him.

Ray, whose last name was Bader was the next to find his room; he nervously smiled as he stood in front of the door and ran his hand across the nameplate. Just as he was promised would happen, the door slid open. Ray poked his head inside before stepping in. After a moment of hesitation, he stepped in and turned to the face Lorraine who remained in the hallway as the door slid closed again, leaving her by herself.

Lorraine, whose last name was Jenkins was the last to find her room; she was nervous and scared at the same time but she did what the rest of the group did and found that everything was consistent with what she had already seen. She ran her hand across the name plate and the door slid open. Lorraine poked her head in the door first. Looking from right to left and back again, she cautiously slipped inside the room. Immediately, the door slid closed.

After a few moments, Dr. Anderson's door slid open and he poked his head out of the room. Nobody was in the hallway so like a 5-year-old sneaking out of his bedroom, past his bedtime, Dr. Anderson crept down the empty hallway toward the O's. He was hoping to see

Robert J Oppenheimer's room. Dr. Anderson wasn't entirely sure how the interlude was going to take place when the opportunity presented itself, but he knew that he was going to have to make the initiation of conversation and be the one to spark up a friendship; if he were to accomplish what it was he had set out to do, regardless of which life his work had started in.

Satisfied that he now knew he was going to be residing next to Oppenheimer's room for minimally a month, Dr. Anderson went back to his room, relaxed and content.

Ray was in his room this entire time. He was so inquisitive with his surroundings that he found himself studying, smelling, and tasting everything.

Ray's room was about 20ft X 15ft; small for living quarters but for a bedroom, was very adequate. The walls were a smooth in texture and eggshell white in color. It was very sterile and clean looking. The bed, a small twin size bed, did not look like much, nor the linens on top of it but was amazingly comfortable when Ray sat down on it. He laid all the way back to test out the bed and see if he could even survive the nights in this rather unique and unbelievable institution.

The bed was pushed long ways up against the wall. There was a window that faced out into the park that the group had been in earlier. The natural light shown (shone) into the room; this made it unnecessary to turn the light fixtures on in the room.

The floor was lined with a grey colored commercial carpet. It was not smooth and soft to the touch, but Ray was confident that it was a far cry from the cold, white tile that lay beneath it.

In the corner of the room, opposite of the door, there was a small bookshelf and desk that was built into the wall. There were some books, brochures and photographs already on it. Ray walked over to the shelf and looked at the photographs. None of the people that he saw in the photos were people that he knew. He thought it to be odd that there would be photographs of complete strangers in his room.

The frames of the photographs had captions written along the bottom. The captions listed people's names. Still, Ray had no idea who these individuals were.

He thumbed through some of the literature that had been neatly located on his desk. Most of it was just maps of the ALPS building. What was interesting though, was that the maps were organized based off location of activities. For instance, instead listing each floor and stating what was located there, the maps were alphabetized based off activity and room, and from there it said what floor that was located on.

Ray just looked at the list, it seemed to go on forever, and the highest floor that he saw as being listed was 56 but he really wasn't sure how many floors there were; mainly, because he stopped reading the maps when his attention was caught to something far more interesting.

A large photo album was located on the desk; it had to be more than 5 inches thick. When Ray opened it, the first page had picture of him. He was astonished to see it, but it was a picture of him at age 31 with his name, Ray Bader written under it.

There were other pictures, all displayed the same way, in fact, and there were hundreds of people. When Ray saw some of the people listed as being family members that he remembered growing up, it suddenly occurred to him that he was in fact holding the family tree photo album. Curious and slowly fitting the pieces together, Ray flipped to the last page of the album. Sure enough, the pictures in the album at the end were the people that were in the photograph frames on the desk. Ray assumed, and this was only a guess based off what Mathew had said earlier, that these are the "living" relatives that they would be united with. Him now being a Therab, or whatever name was assigned to this group of special individuals, made him curious on the future dynamics that were in store for him.

Lorraine was sitting on the edge of her bed. She rocked back and forth in panic. She felt helpless, trapped, and had no idea what to do.

Her room was set up exactly like Ray's room, the only difference of course, was the people in her photographs and the photographs in the album found on her desk.

Now though, neither piqued her interest, not even the map of the building. Her thoughts were jumbled, and she did not know what to do. All she did was continue to try to rationalize the entire situation and recognize the distinct possibility that everything she had thought was real in her former life, was not. Lorraine had never felt lonelier and more scared. Furthermore, could not figure out why she felt as if she were the only one that was visibly upset by this entire situation. Did that mean that everyone else was in on it and this was just some kind of sick but elaborate practical joke?

Lorraine got up once and looked out the window that faced into the same park as Ray's window. For a moment, she lost herself in the beauty and splendor of the clean, lush scenery. Surely, she was not living the same life as before because even she knew that the world did not exist in such a perfect state.

She could tell that she was a few stories off the ground but did not know how far up. But as she peered down into the park, she was immediately startled back to the assumed reality that she temporarily left as she gazed upon the wonderfully cultivated landscape. An individual was standing down in the park; he looked like he was dressed as an orderly, but Lorraine could not be sure what his function at the facility really was. Lorraine watched this individual for a few moments, then, and she would be willing to bet her life on it, she and this person locked eyes in one another's gaze. That astonished Lorraine simply because of the remote possibility of their eyes meeting at such a distance.

Lorraine stared and the man started back. In an alarming and menacing manner, the orderly looking man began smiling at Lorraine. He exposed a mouthful of teeth that to her, looked pointy and animal-like. Something about the way he was looking at her made her feel very uneasy. So uneasy that she immediately broke the locked gaze and removed herself from the window so that he could not see her anymore.

Not wanting to believe what her eyes told her just happened, Lorraine poked her head up to the far corner of the window and peered out. Even though she knew it was physically impossible, she almost expected him to be right there in the window, somehow floating in the air and hovering at her window, but he was not. In fact, he was no longer looking up at her window when she peeked back down toward him. Maybe she had imagined the whole thing. Maybe she only thought he was looking at her.

Lorraine sat herself back down at the edge of the bed. She continued to ignore the maps, the photographs, and the album on her desk. She did not spend any time looking around. She just sat there and rocked back and forth.

Dr. Anderson had no issue with making himself at home. He went thru all the drawers in the desk. He tested the window to see how it opened, removed the vent covers that were in the wall. Essentially, he behaved as though he was a prison inmate, and he was trying to figure out what he would have to do should he need to escape.

He read through the entire map within 15 minutes. Inside the desk drawers, he had found some paper and pens so as he was reading, he took notes. He made notations of where all the libraries were located as well as the fact that there were numerous "stores" located within the ALPS building. Although he was not sure what exactly was used as currency, he was pleased to see that the "stores" were sectioned off from one another based off of the product that they "sold". Dr. Anderson made a note to ask Matthew about these stores and what was used as currency, he underlined this note twice. He then made notes of where hardware stores were, and lumber stores were. He was confident that him finding a store for explosives was remote. However, Dr. Anderson also knew that many normal household products could be used in lieu of actual explosives; the trick was to just figure out what had what characteristics. That is where the library would become very handy. Dr. Anderson was a very resourceful individual and when properly motivated, could make the best out of any situation.

His excitement and eagerness permeated the room. When he had completed his note taking, he put the piece of paper and the pen in the inner breast pocket of his sports coat. He got up and started to walk around the room. He took notice of any odors, sounds, inconsistencies in the structure. Walking past a mirror, Dr. Anderson stopped dead in his tracks and gazed at the mirror. He smiled in a devilish way when he saw the reflection that was looking back at him.

The reflection showed a younger version of him. He looked like he could not have been more than 30 years old. It was a comical sight though to say the least. The young chap that looked back at him looked like a man child dressed in his grandfather's clothes. Still wearing his clothes from his previous life, Dr. Anderson, or the new, younger version of himself was wearing the white, button up dress shirt covered by a grey, hounds tooth sport jacket. The kind that had the leather patches on the elbows. Simply put, Dr. Anderson looked like he was playing dress up and the site greatly amused him.

Dr. Anderson, not wanting to wait for the announcement from Matthew to be delivered like they were a bunch of cattle being rounded up for grub, let himself out of his room and began walking in the direction of the lobby that they had been in when Matthew dismissed them for a break.

Dr. Anderson walked down the hallway with such confidence, you would have thought he had been there for years and knew exactly where he was going and what he was doing. But that was just him; he never embarked on anything with caution. He figured that it was always best to look confident, be assertive and never let anybody know your weaknesses or downfalls.

He arrived back at the lobby and saw a few random individuals walking around but nobody from the group he was expecting to meet there. That did not matter to him though. He strolled outside and took in the warm, clean air. Basting in the sun, Dr. Anderson waited for the rest of the group to arrive.

After only 5 minutes, a voice came on the loudspeaker and announced that Ray Bader, Lorraine Jenkins and John Anderson were to report back to the main lobby. Dr. Anderson mumbled the word doctor under his breath in an annoyed tone. Not that he was pompous, but he did work extremely hard to earn the title of doctor and just simply preferred to be addressed as such.

Dr. Anderson lingered a few more minutes outside before reentering the building. When he got back in, both Lorraine and Ray were standing there. He saw Matthew entering the lobby from a different hallway and waived everyone over to him as he did so.

Blindly following, all three approached Matthew. He instructed everyone, "Lunch will be served in a buffet manner in a large room referred to as The Chimera Room. The food will be served for 2 hours, from 12-2 pm every day. It will be closed for preparation of dinner and open back up at 5. It would be open until 7pm then remain closed until the following morning where it would be opened again from 8-10 am." Matthew then went on to say, "All of this information is found in the brochures, handbooks and maps that everyone should have found on their desk but don't let that ever deter you from asking questions. Oh, and if you have any specific food allergies, it is up to you to set up a meeting with the head chef and nutritionist for specific food instructions and menus. Again though, the names of those individuals and any other administrative personnel can be found in the brochures and/or handbooks."

Matthew turned from the group and began walking back down the hallway he had just arrived from saying, "Now if everyone will follow me, I'm sure that you are all very hungry."

The group walked briefly before Matthew made a 90 deg turn into a double doorway. The doorway led into a massive room that was filled with all kinds of tasty aromas. The room was bright, and the ceiling was one massive sky light. There were green plants all over the place. The cafeteria or Chimera Room looked like a massive atrium, decorated with tables, benches and chairs.

The room was filled with a low murmur from the conversations going on amongst the others in there. Kiosks were located all over the massive room. Each one seemed to serve a different entrée.

People were roaming around from group of people to group of people. They all seemed to mingle together and laugh together. It looked like a weird utopia that Ray, Lorraine, and Dr. Anderson suddenly belonged to.

The aromas that filled the noses of the three newcomers instantly made their stomachs react in a lively manner. None of them knew where to start or what food they wanted to eat. Feeling overwhelmed and awe struck, the three stood in the doorway and continued to stare at the sight. Not wanting to miss a single option by deciding too hastily, the three remained still.

Premonition – Volume 6

For a moment, nobody said anything then Lorraine looked at Ray and said, "I'm not even really that hungry."

"Me neither," he replied. "It's weird, we all have been awakened almost 3000 years later and everyone else seems to be ok with it all. Why doesn't anyone else seem to be, I do not know, apprehensive? Scared? Why is it only just us?"

Dr. Anderson straightened his back as he seemed to have located exactly what it was that he was looking for because he replied, in a much-callused tone, "Maybe it's just the 2 of you. I kind of like the idea of being brought back. Especially with others that I would never have had the honor of meeting in the past." With that last comment, Dr. Anderson walked away from Ray and Lorraine and head straight to the food kiosk that Robert Oppenheimer was standing at helping himself to a plate of what looked like fruits. Those fruits though were none that Dr. Anderson had ever seen before.

Despite his lack of familiarity, he grabbed a plate and began loading the food onto his plate. He looked at Robert and smiled saying, "Looks good doesn't it?"

Ray and Lorraine were watching him the entire time, "What do you think that guy is up to?" Ray asked Lorraine as he nodded in Dr. Anderson's direction.

"I'm honestly not sure," Lorraine replied. "He seems very, I don't know what the word is but like he's got an ulterior motive.

"Yea," Ray agreed, "That's the same feeling that I get. Where are you from anyway?"

"Iowa," she replied. "You?"

"Los Angeles. What do you think about all of this?" Ray asked motioning with his head to the room in front of them.

"I'm not sure. They did not talk about any of this in Sunday school, that is for sure.

"Do you think it's real?" She asked.

"Certainly, feels real but just as real as it feels, it doesn't feel right," he replied.

"Do you remember how you, you know," she stopped and paused as though she was searching for the right word to use."

Ray looked at her and, in an effort, to try to help here out, offered up "Died?"

"Yes," she whispered. "I mean, if in fact this is what happened to us?

"Well," he began. I remember going for a walk and then hearing squealing tires and then this sensation of, I guess I would call it flying. But after that, all I remember is waking up in, what did they call it? The FX4 cell. What about you?"

"Not much," she shrugged. She motioned for Ray and her to sit down in some white wicker chairs that had red striped cushions in them. They both took a seat, and she began again, "I know that I had been sick for a long time. Kidneys." She rolled her eyes and shook her hands in a manner to suggest that she felt the illness was more of a nuisance than something she suffering she had to endure. "Then I remember being upstairs doing the laundry and I guess that was about it. I can't remember anything else."

"3000 years seems a bit far-fetched don't you think?" Ray asked as he relaxed back into the chair. "I mean, there is something really familiar and not that different, but I can't really put my finger on it. But then again, how could they have known anything about the people that were in the photo album? I mean, I guess that's information that could've been shared to help with this, hoax."

"Is that what you think this is?" Lorraine asked. "One big hoax?"

"Well," he began, "what else could it be?"

"Do you know what Salvation is?" Lorraine asked him. "Or at least, what is it to you?"

"Well," Ray began as he tilted his head back and looked up. The ceiling of the Chimera Room was a sky mural. It looked so real at first. The blue of the sky was the perfect shade and seemed to go on forever. The clouds billowed across the canvas landscape. For a moment, he felt like he was outside. Then, to his surprise, he felt a slight breeze move through the room and literally saw it cascade across the clouds sending a slight ripple effect. This small, almost unnoticeable event sent a wave of shock down his spine as he shook his head back to reality. "Wait, what? I'm sorry Lorraine, what did you say?"

"I didn't say anything," she replied. "You were about to tell me what Salvation was to you."

"Right, well, I think that Salvation is being delivered to the place that you are destined to be. I guess I believe that it is different for everyone, you know. For me, I think that it is a place that will always remind me of my mom. She died when I was a kid and so if I found the place that would allow me to be with her, I would feel complete. It would be my Salvation; the place I was destined to be delivered to. What about you?"

"I think that it's the place where our soul is destined to be delivered to. I do not think that we are supposed to know where or how we will find our Salvation. I mean," and it was obvious that she was trying to tread carefully and not downplay his thoughts about his mother and his desire to be with her. "But let me put it like this. I believe that each person is created for an awfully specific reason. A reason that we are not aware of or will ever know. It is like being a piece of a puzzle, a big puzzle but you are so small, you never really see the big picture. I believe that Salvation is seeing that big picture."

"Are you talking about the meaning life," Ray asked.

"No, meaning implies one static moment in time. I think that when we see this big puzzle," she said in a tone that suggested she was trying to find a better word but just couldn't, "we see what we were destined to be a part of. And it changes you know? I think that God adds puzzle pieces all the time, there are countless pieces and each one impacts another differently."

"I'm not sure that I follow," Ray said glancing at her over his shoulder.

"Well, let us say that my puzzle piece, for lack of better words is green. My Salvation might show me that I am in fact part of a bush. As the years go on, I would then see that I am part of a thicket. As more years go on, I would see that I am part of a forest. And the bush, the thicket and the forest are all something to something else. Get it?"

"Yea," he said, "I think I do. Interesting." He smiled, "That's a lot deeper than my definition but then again, I was never really the religious type. So, since your theory has clarity and holds more water than mine, how do you reconcile this place?"

"I'm not sure yet," she said, frankly. "It's not exactly falling in line with what I was taught to believe and to be even more frank, it's very unsettling to know that 1. We are going to be put in front of our loved ones which goes against God's plan and 2. That an entire alternative life and existence was created by man. Again, against God's plan."

"How do you know that all of this is against God's plan," Ray asked. "I'm a doubting man by nature but I do believe in God; my doubts come from organized religion and organized religion is where we learn what we think is God's will."

"No," she said as she stood up, "I don't believe that God intended on any of this." She motioned for Ray to get up and follow her. He did and the two walked from food kiosk to food kiosk looking at the oddities served up to them. There were foods that they could not even begin to describe. The colors and textures varied but all were never naturally occurring fruits, vegetables or whatever type of plant life they evolved to be as they were seen that day.

"What is this?" Lorraine pointed at a bright blue pineapple is what first came to mind."

The orderly, looking up at her smiled. The smile sent a shiver down her spine as it was the same toothy, grinning orderly that she saw before.

"Mum, why this is a thrimbarb," he replied with the same toothy grin.

Lorraine cleared her throat in discomfort and asked, "Where do thrimbarbs come from?"

"Well," he began in voice that spoke with an 'I'm so glad you asked' tone, "thrimbarbs were cross bred between fruits of 3 hypotenuse planetary system. The soil from all 3 planets were mixed along with the gases from the 3 planets and then Voila! Instant thrimbarbs! They are quite delicious. Sweet and full of nectar! Nectar is good for the body and soul." His voice was overly exaggerated, almost like a used car salesman's voice.

"What is 3 hypotenuse planetary system?" Lorraine asked as she eyed the thrimbarb up and down.

"Well, you probably know it as the Belt of Orion on Earth. Each of the 3 stars you would see from your planet, when looking at it from another is actually1 of many that are all in alignment. The aligned stars are all a hypotenuse of the same triangle."

"That doesn't even make any sense," Ray offered up. "There is only 1 hypotenuse on a triangle."

"Well young man, it is amazing how we decide what is real and what isn't real when in our lifetimes, we only see the world from 1 vantage point isn't it? I would expect that the more opportunities we have to view from different perspectives, they more open we might become to things we thought not possible," The orderly's eyes twinkled in amusement.

Dr. Anderson invited Robert Oppenheimer a seat next to him. He chose a window seat where he was able to view exterior grounds of the ALPS building. "So," Dr. Anderson began, "I too am a doctor, I specialize in medicine and have a great deal of interest in the reanimation of human tissue. It would appear though, that the world has gone on without me as I have a lot learning to do in order to catch up," he chuckled heartily as he began to cut up something on his plate that he had no idea what it was nor did he intend on eating it.

"It seems so," Robert replied with the same hearty chuckle. The dialogue was so forced that an outsider listening in might very well had expected the next comment to be, "Good show old man!"

Dr. Anderson, intrigued by the very theory of tissue reanimation as well as the new advanced concepts that Mathew had mentioned, specifically the idea about the human body being a giant capacitor of type, took down notes feverishly. "So, your creation of the atom bomb began quite a stir in our time didn't it?" He had no idea where the conversation was going and since his interest really was not to become friends with Robert Oppenheimer, he really did not care how socially awkward he was coming across.

"I beg your pardon?" Robert asked appalled.

"Oh, I just mean that with World War 2 and then the Soviet Red scare, the United States really put themselves on the map in terms of superior intellect and application," Dr. Anderson said in a nonchalant attitude.

"Well," Robert began with a more level tone, "I suppose that we did however, there were and I suspect still are a great deal of people that believed that type of power never should have been discovered." He rolled his eyes back as he stuck a fork full of whatever it was, he was eating into his mouth and said, "Now I have become Death, the destroyer of worlds."

Dr. Anderson laughed out loud, "A bit theatrical don't you think?"

Robert opened his eyes and with a distinct look of distaste, not for the food but rather Dr. Anderson's company without a doubt, "Sir, we are men of science yes? We solve problems to improve man kind and deliver the power of enlightenment. I have delivered no enlightenment, nor have I improved mankind. What I have in fact delivered is a tool that when used by the wrong people, can destroy us all. There is one thing that we as humans have proven repeatedly, we are never content with what we have. We always want more. We wanted all of Europe and Asia until we arrived here in the America's and once, we ate up all the land here, we still wanted more. Look where we've gone now." He laughed again as he waived his hands in the air, fork in one hand and a knife in the other, "my friend, we've apparently gone intergalactic. What is next? Pursuance of the 4th dimension?"

"Precisely," Dr. Anderson said as leaned in forward to talk in a more discreet tone. I believe that you and I, if we work together can break down the barriers that say we are dead when we die."

"Well, my friend, it seems as though someone beat you to the punch. Here we are," Robert said as he gestured to the room.

"No, I mean back then. I mean taking what we know here and using it back then. I am talking about having the power to have never lost your loved ones back then. If we had the knowledge then that we have now, maybe there would never have to be a now and we would always remain in the then."

"In the then? Anderson, you are talking like a madman. I am sorry old man; I am accepting things exactly as how they have been handed to me. I am reanimated, as a new race of species apparently but none the less, this is my destiny; this was what was to be, and I am ok with that. Now, I appreciate your admiration for my work, but I must insist that you go elsewhere and let me be."

"But your theory on the black hole, aren't you even the slightest bit curious? What if we were to use your discoveries about atomic fission? What if we discovered that the black hole really is not a black hole at all? What if,"

Robert put his hand up in a clear gesture that he no longer wanted to hear what Dr. Anderson had to say. "Sir, I'm old, I'm tired, I do not seek any more knowledge than what I have acquired and what I have acquired, I've published and taught for my predecessors to take over. And if this place is as real as it feels, I'm going to bow my head as they seem to have made leaps and bounds from when I was, oh dear, what do they refer to them as? The Plerab Race?"

Lorraine and Ray allowed the orderly, even though his behavior was quite odd, to place a thrimbarb on their plates. It was about 4 inches in diameter and almost looked like a blue kiwi. They went back to their wicker chairs but before doing so, grabbed what they could only assume to be a cup of coffee.

Lorraine took a sip from her coffee cup and then looked down at her plate in disgust, "I can't eat this," she said as she placed it down on the table in front of them. "I have no idea what it is."

Ray shrugged and cut off a small piece with the side of his fork. He pierced it and held it up to his nose, "It smells sweet, almost like strawberries." He put the fork in his mouth and chewed. "It's weird, I can't describe the texture. It is chewy, like gum because it does not seem to break down even though you chew more and more. But it tastes good. You should try some Lori."

Her eyes darted in his direction in the instant that the last bit of breath exhaled from his mouth as he uttered an abbreviated version of her name. "What's the matter?" Ray asked genuinely confused.

"My husband called me that," was all she said.

"Lorraine, I'm sorry. I just assumed that Lori was a normal nickname that you would have been called. I didn't mean anything by it," Ray said apologetically.

"It's ok Ray," she said warmly as she sat her plate down. "I know you didn't. I think I am going to go back to my room. I feel a bit tired and I think that a little rest will do me some good."

"But you haven't eaten anything," Ray protested. "At least eat a little bit of," he laughed, "Whatever the hell this is. For all you know we could be asked to climb Mount Everest later today."

Lorraine nodded and sat back down. She was a reasonable woman and even though part of her felt like either this wasn't real or they were no longer even on planet Earth let alone later on possibly traversing the mountainous sides of Mount Everest, she was mildly curious on exactly what the thrimbarb tasted like. Even if this was a dream. Even if she were like Dorothy in Oz and Ray was her Toto. That brought a small smile to her face when thinking about it? She wondered who would be her Wicked Witch? Was it Dr. Anderson? More importantly though, where were her red ruby slippers? How would she get home?

She bit down and an explosion of flavor and juice filled her mouth. It really was delectable, and she could never deny that. "What a

vivid sensation for a dream," she thought to herself as she continued to
chew.

A Theological Discussion – Volume 7

Lorraine used the palm of her hand to open the door to her room like she had been instructed. She was tired, not physically tired but not emotionally tired either. She felt tired in a sense that there was something beyond her that was telling her she needed to be tired and that she needed to lie down.

She kept thinking back to the conversation that her and Ray were having about Salvation. She knew that what she was telling him was what she knew she wanted to believe but she also knew that sometimes, there are things that we want to believe but deep down, we just do not. She wondered where all of this stood with her. At first, as she sat down on the bed, she kind of laughed to herself and thought, "You silly, you believe exactly what it is that you choose to believe. You are inside your own head right now. There is no peer pressure, if they even have that at your age, or media or anything else to challenge or dispel what you want to believe. So why are you questioning yourself?"

The thought seemed so real and so tangible that she would have bet her life on the fact that there was a real live conversation going on in that room. But it was just her and it made her even more confused.

She felt like she was standing in front of a mirror which was placed in front of another mirror, so the reflection would go on and on, forever.

Lorraine laid down on the bed and wondered, in addition to her other wonderments, if the weird fruit that she ate had psychedelic properties. She had always been a very pragmatic person with a touch of curiosity but even these thoughts were enough for her to take pause and collect her bearings.

As she silently thought about the type of person that she was, her eyelids became very heavy and she drifted off to sleep, or so she thought.

Lorraine's eyes fluttered as she heard the soft sound of someone knocking at her door.

Still groggy and unsure of how long she had been asleep, Lorraine got up out of bed and went to the door. When she opened it, Matthew, the gentleman who facilitated the orientation the day prior, was standing in front of her. "Lorraine, there is someone here to see you," he said with a smile that could not only be seen on his face but could clearly be heard in his voice as well. Matthew stepped off to the side and from behind him stepped a middle-aged woman dressed in a simple, red gingham house dress. Lorraine's mouth dropped open as she loudly gasped at the woman standing in front of her. The woman smiled a soft, demure smile as she said, "Hello Lorraine; my little 'Rainy." The woman stretched out her arms to embrace Lorraine.

Lorraine blinked back the tears as she whispered, "Mama, is it really you?" Lorraine had lost her mother when she was only 14 years old, or when Bethany was 31 years old to be exact. Bethany, Lorraine's mother had died from kidney failure; the same affliction that Lorraine had presumed that she died from. "It is my baby girl," Bethany embraced her adult child that she had never seen before; she embraced Lorraine as though they had never parted in the first place.

Bethany was a very petite woman. She had long, silky blonde hair that was peppered with strands of silver. Her face was youthful and her skin pale white like porcelain. She was exactly how Lorraine had remembered her all those years ago.

Lorraine could feel her entire body tremble in her mother's arms. An achy feeling that she only vaguely remembered started to swirl in the pit of her stomach. At first, she did not know what the feeling was; she did not recognize it. But the harder she squeezed her mother, as if she would never see her again, she remembered what it was. It was the dull, empty feeling that she felt for a long time after her mother had passed. That lost feeling of running into the house after school to share in amazement and horror, that you had started your first period at school. That disappointing feeling of having a crush on a boy at school and coming home only to know your only confidant would by your diary. The empty feeling of knowing that you would be deprived of a best friend when you became a grown woman.

Lorraine shuttered as all these feelings came back in one massive swoosh that nearly knocked the wind right out of her. She had blocked out the pain for so long, she almost forgot what it felt like. She remembered now; she remembered and she wished that she hadn't because somewhere, deep inside, she knew that she would have to go through this all over again and that pain, that inconsolable pain would relentlessly hammer down on her again. The pain of losing a loved one; the pain of acknowledging that they had reached a point in time when they would never speak nor embrace each other again.

"I'll let you two be then," Matthew said as he closed the door to Lorraine's room.

The two women let go for a moment and just stood and stared at each other. "You've become such a beautiful woman Rainy; you really have."

"I've not heard anyone call me Rainy in years Mama! Nobody but you," she said with a warm smile. "You look exactly how I remember you."

The two women walked to the bed and sat down next to one another. Bethany clasped her hands around Lorraine's and sighed, "I've missed you so much honey. How long have you been here?"

Lorraine shrugged and said, "Since yesterday. Mama, this place is weird. What is it?"

Bethany sighed and thought before she replied, "I don't know dear. I have been here for about 17 years now and every day seems like it is the first. To tell you the truth, I cannot remember a week ago, a year ago, or anything. The only thing that I can remember was the first day; everything after that is a blur."

"Well," Lorraine hesitated, "then how do I know you're my Mama? What if none of this is real?"

Bethany took Lorraine's hand and placed it across her heart. She smiled and said, "We are the same my darling, my blood is in you and my heart is yours, I am absolutely sure that my being here as your mama is real."

Larraine smiled and nodded.

"This place though," Bethany continued on, that I'm not too sure about."

"That's what I mean" Lorraine said, "All of this, what does it mean? Therabs and Plerabs? This is absurd! But if it were absurd, then I wouldn't be sitting here talking with you."

Bethany smiled and put her finger to her daughter's lips silencing her. She took a deep breath and began, "Well, let us look at this, I mean all of this. Let us look at this objectively."

Lorraine was hesitant at first, she did not know what her mother meant, "Ok."

"Let us look at this realistically and theologically. First, from the realistic standpoint," Bethany began. "We are in a place that allegedly exists almost 3000 years into the future. Does time go that far? I would say yes, realistically, time never stops; so yes 3000 years into the future could and very well would exist. Brining people back to life as a new race, presumably at age 31? That part I am not too sure about. The first question is, why would you do that?

"Well," Lorraine began, "At 31 years old, you are at your prime. You are still strong; you are experienced, and you still feel that there is plenty to live for."

Her mother nodded in agreement and asked, "And why would this be important?"

"That's the part that doesn't make a lot of sense," Lorrain sighed. "Assuming that is the reason that we are brought back, what are we in our prime for? What are we eager to live for?"

"Well, let's skip then over to the theological aspect of this," Bethany suggested.

"Ok," Lorraine concentrated. "Faith tells us that when we die, we are judged before the almighty Lord and presumably, then find out whether we go to Heaven or Hell. If we accept Christ as our Lord and Savior, we will go to Heaven. But if that belief structure were true, then we would not be here. We would have found salvation and idea of bringing us back or the concept of reanimation of dead tissue just wouldn't exist."

"But" Bethany began, "We are here. I am here with you and theologically speaking, I should not be."

"Should or could not be here," Lorraine asked.

"That's a good question," Bethany agreed as she validated Lorraine's point. "There are a lot of things people can do, but that doesn't mean that they should do. If you have discovered the science behind tissue reanimation, should you pursue it? What are the consequences? Just because you do not believe in God, Heaven or Hell, does that mean that they do not exist? Here's my question," Bethany straightened up as though she wanted to make sure that what she was about to say she wanted to make sure was very clear, "I love you Lorraine, so very much but this," she pointed to herself and Lorraine, "And us being together like this, in this place, I do not believe is what God wanted. These people are depriving us from our salvation because of their lack faith. They believe that science and scientific advancements prove that God does not exist. I have heard so many people, people that have been brought back, if there was a God, this would not be possible. But here is the thing Lorraine, it goes back to free will. God gave us the ability to discern for ourselves what is right or wrong. God gave us the ability to choose for ourselves what we thought was the will of God. I have heard so many discuss so many topics in the last 17 years. They talk of war, murder, abortion, cloning and so many more. People believe that they can substitute the existence of God by justifying what they feel they are entitled to have; be it as humans, men, and women. What if they are entitled to all those things and more, but are choosing to exercise those entitlements incorrectly and against God's will?"

"I think I see where you're going with this," Lorraine said thoughtfully. "For example, if a woman feels that she has the right to do with her body what she feels is her business, she's absolutely correct however; it's God's will for her as a woman to have control over her body but if she chooses to behave immoral, then she's taking a gift that was God's will and choosing to abuse that gift?"

"Something along those lines," Bethany agreed nodding.

"So, what about abortion?" Lorraine asked.

"What about it," Bethany opened her hands to welcome the discussion.

"Well there are a lot of people, both men and women that feel abortion is wrong no matter what, well what about the women who are victims of sex crimes and become pregnant?"

Bethany paused and then just smiled softly saying, "Babies are a gift from God; no matter how they were conceived. To abort a baby because of the circumstances under which it was born is just selfish of the mother."

"What do you mean selfish?" Lorraine asked.

"Selfish because she is putting her own needs and wants above the value of a life; granted a life that she must bear against her will because it wasn't part of her plan but it was part of God's plan and who are we to question God's plan. We don't have to like it, we don't have to agree with it, but we must endure it," Bethany explained. "This whole thing," she gestured around in a way that clearly suggested she meant beyond the room they were in, "is so much bigger than us and to kill off a life that God intended to walk this earth is a crime against our Lord."

"Ok, well speaking of crimes, what about things like war?" Lorraine inquired.

"Well," Bethany began, "The way that I see it, intent is in the heart and no matter what you say or do, you can never deceive what's truly in your heart. So, if you are going into war with a heart full of hate, you are not fulfilling God's will. Conversely, if you go into war with love in your heart and your only desire is to liberate those that are being persecuted, God will allow you to atone for your actions necessary at the time. But again," Bethany held up her finger as a gesture to remind caution, "Only as long as the actions you committed against mankind were not enjoyed and were not done out of hate but rather necessity."

"So how does this place fit into your theory?" Lorraine inquired

"Well," Bethany began, "It doesn't really fit anywhere yet."

"Why not," Lorraine asked.

"Because we don't know what's in here," she pointed to Lorraine's heart. "We don't know why this place exists yet, but I do have a theory."

"If in fact it exists," Lorraine added.

"Exactly," Bethany agreed.

"So how do we find out why this place exists and why we were presumably brought back 3000 years later? I mean, what is your theory?" Lorraine asked.

"Let's circle back to the beginning of this discussion," Bethany said. "The realistic approach and mindset. Every science advancement that has been made over the centuries has done one thing, gotten us further away from God and placed us a little higher each time on the pedestal that we are gently removing God from."

"Ok, and also the idea that just because we can do something doesn't mean we should it; we have to be honest first with what's in our hearts," Lorraine added.

"Right," Bethany agreed, "So the last notion that applies heavily to this situation is that the greatest trick the devil ever played on mankind was for mankind to not believe he existed. If the devil does not exist, then neither does God; one cannot exist without the other."

"Ok, I'm not sure that I follow," Lorrain said.

"This entire place represents an entire existence against God's will and yet, there is no brimstone and fire, there is no eternal flame of damnation, there is not hooved goat man standing before us with a pitch fork; so maybe there is no Hell and if there is no Hell," Bethany paused.

"There is no Heaven," Lorraine finished for her.

"Exactly," Bethany said. "So, you have a huge race of people that now believe that Heaven and Hell do not exist and by right, would proclaim themselves to be living proof, the Therab race.

"Right, but you also have the Plerab race who are living proof that life will still find a way; as it represents God's will," Lorraine added.

"So, if you had one race of people believing one specific idea and another race of people believing another idea, what do you suppose is going to happen?" Bethany asked.

"One group is going to try to convince the other group of the validity behind their idea," Lorraine said. "And if the validity of one idea is substantiated by a reality around them, it'll hold more water in the eyes of the skeptical." Lorraine thought for a moment and tried to reconcile what her and her mother just analyzed and presumably concluded in their minds. She then started, "So the in the end, why do the Therabs care if the Plerabs believe in God or not?"

"It's not the Therabs, it's those who created the Therabs. The Therabs are just a tool used to get the Plerabs to believe," Bethany explained.

"Ok, so why?" Lorraine persisted.

"Because it's the money from the Plerabs that is going to the creators of the Therabs. The more they can convince the world that God doesn't exist, the more power they will assume."

"And what is it that they are after?" Lorraine asked.

"Power, control, domination; any of those things are my guess. They are creating a world that exists how they think it should exist. They are creating a race of people that they believe emulate how an individual should look and behave. The irony is, they try hard to defy that God exists when they in fact are trying to be God."

The Social Control – Volume 8

Dr. Anderson continued sitting at the table with Dr. Oppenheimer for a moment longer before he pushed his chair back and got up. His actions had a slight aggression in them that communicated that he was clearly frustrated with where the conversation was going. "Well sir," Dr. Anderson said with an obvious tone, "I believe you and I have a different thirst for science and the pursuance of it, I don't see my thirst ever being quenched regardless of how the world views my discoveries."

Dr. Oppenheimer smiled as he set his fork down on his plate and picked up his napkin from his lap. He dabbed the corners of his mouth and said, "Sir, the legend of Pandora's Box has been told for centuries and that is because the message stands true regardless of the age you live in. That message is that some things are left unfound and undisturbed." Dr. Oppenheimer nodded in Dr. Anderson's direction to clearly indicate that he was done with the conversation.

Dr. Anderson nodded back to give the same indication and turned on his heal and walked away. "Foolish old man," he grumbled under breath.

Dr. Anderson made his way the entrance of the Chimera Room and turned around to look at the occupants. He felt defeated and like he had hit a wall. He was hopeful that Dr. Oppenheimer would share in his enthusiasm and together they would piece together the scientific advancements of the last 3000 years. He had always thought that the love of science was something that you did not just get tired of. It was not a job; it was the insatiable quest for the answer always asked, "Why does this happen?"

What he wasn't expecting was a dried up old man who used to be one of the scientific leaders in his day now become someone that chooses to ignore that he is actually having a conversation 3000 years after his death and would rather sit and eat some kind of fruit hybrid.

John stood at the entrance to the room and began wondering the chronology and the reason behind the chronology. "If Dr. Oppenheimer died in 1967, what is the significance behind bringing him back in the year 4883?" he thought out loud in a whisper. That question did not sit well with John at all and he began to suspect that there was a lot more Dr. Oppenheimer than John had thought. He doubted very seriously that it was just pure happenstance that one of greatest scientists he had admired in his days of collegiate study happened to be regenerated in the very year, location and facility that he was in. John never believed in coincidences, he believed in premeditated situations and decisions that one was simply unaware of at the time.

John left the Chimera room and instead of going back to the main lobby, movement caught his eye and he saw a long, dimly light corridor that was narrow and went on forever it seemed. Curiosity of course getting the better part of him, he decided to follow the corridor. The motion that had caught his eye was not distinct. It was more like shadowy movement that would interfere and disrupt the continuous flow light. It had a greenish-blue tint to it which is what caught John's attention to begin with.

He walked softly down the hallway trying to remain as light footed as possible. The floor the corridor was a high gloss tile that was slate gray in color with black colored grout.

The walls were an industrial, steel gray in color that were smooth dry walled texture. The lighting above him was a very dim line of recessed florescent bulbs. They were much dimmer than the greenish-blue light that was at, what he presumed, to be the end of the corridor.

John could here murmuring coming from the distance and it grew louder as he approached the source from where the greenish-blue light came from.

The corridor ended at a fork where there was a room off to the right and off to the left. The room off to the left was empty and dark but the room off to the right was where the odd green light shown from.

John peaked his head around the corner and saw a small gathering of people.

They were seated at a table in a way that created a full square. The people seated at the table were forced to face one another which created an optimal discussion setting; nobody was at the head of the table or discussion which led one to believe that nobody was presumably over anyone else.

John held his breath as he recoiled his head and just listened to the discussion

"This is absurd," he heard a man exclaim. "We're having a hard-enough time trying to convince anyone that there is merit behind what we are doing."

"And what is that merit Peter?" a woman asked.

"It's to prove with absolute certainty that there is no God. Do you know how many lives we could save from mass genocide brought on by battles that stem from theological disputes? People killing each other in mases to show that their faith is right and just."

"Ok," the woman, John assumed to be the same one before, "So what? Faith and spiritual devotion are the driving force behind kindness and generosity, so if you remove the faith and the spirituality, won't people innately want to become more cynical, greedy and self-absorbed? I mean the whole concept of salvation and redemption are thrown out the window, right? Plus, not to mention other factors that create division and hatred, ethnicity, gender, sexual orientation, on and on."

"Not necessarily," she paused before continuing. "The entire concept of good behavior being rewarded whether in a spiritual afterlife or otherwise still applies."

"How do you propose we do this on a larger scale then? What are your controls? What are your variables, hypothetically of course?"

Susan cleared here throat before she began, "We approach it as a 3 phase project gentlemen. The first phase has already begun. Right now, we have a secluded building that is housing approximately 50,000 subjects that believe that they were brought back to life and are living in an age 3000 years later. We did that by controlling their senses, introducing hybrid foods, had them interact with people who were long thought to be deceased but were in fact either body doubles or holograms when we were able to use that. The illusion of tissue reanimation has already been established. Now we move onto the second phase. We introduce the concept of selection. We did this by creating in their minds, 2 different races, the Therabs and the Plerabs. The Therabs now believe that they are the superior race because they've undergone this transition of being reanimated. They believe that they are stronger, healthier and immune. They will then believe that the Plerabs are the inferior race. They will be viewed as being nothing more than contagious, disease carrying free thinkers that are a heavy weight on society. The third and final phase is infiltration. We release the 50,000 subjects back into society and let them spread the concept with the intent of funneling people through this process we have created and allowing them then to emerge under the belief that they are now a new race of person. They will preach their truth and it will be received by many because the Therabs will be living and talking proof that what they are saying is true. We do this over and over again in the same format until we've created one homogeneous race who is set with a predisposition to be genetically defined by the attributes we've hand selected"

"What about the skeptics, there will be a lot who think this is complete rubbish and honestly, if I were them, I would agree."

Susan started again, "Many are blind followers and will subscribe without question. Many more are going to be incentivized by their own personal gain so all we have to do is figure out what motivates them, and they'll come."

"What about those that are sick, dying, deformed, mental health issues. Pre-existing conditions that would prove or disprove, I should say, that the Therabs do not actually exist?"

"We wait list them and let them die. They will spend their last day thinking that their time will soon be coming, and their immortality is within hand's reach."

John heard one-man chuckle and added, "This is a tricky game you're going to play Susan, but I like it."

John started to hear feet shuffling to suggest to him that the people sitting at the table were moving around a bit; possibly getting ready to leave. He turned quickly and half ran, and half walked back down the corridor that he came from.

John went back to his room and sat down on the bed. He thought for a moment then went to his dresser where his little notebook lay neatly on the dresser top. John started jotting down notes but used code words instead. He had always been a bit paranoid, but this place made him completely on edge.

His code words were nonsensical in that, they would mean nothing to someone coming upon his notebook and would probably read as nothing more than gibberish. He used words like beef stew to describe the collection of people that he stumbled upon at the end of the corridor. He used phrases like sugar versus sweetener to describe the difference between the Therabs and the Plerabs. Ultimately what he was trying to do was figure out what the conversation was about. He sat on the edge of his bed and started drawing lines from one group to the other. He made notes about common traits from one group to the other. He questioned the turmoil that the group was vocalizing, and the question posed, does God exist or not. John stared at his notes for a while and thought. He kept going back to the original question that was plaguing him and that was, "why here and why now?"

John returned the notebook to his dresser top; he paused for a moment and then changed his mind and opened the top drawer and hid the notebook inside one of his socks. He paused a minute further and decided that it's best to just sit on this information for the time being, he really concluded that he had no choice but to keep it to himself, he hadn't a sole to confide in at this point and even if he did, he's not entirely sure that he knows what he has overheard.

Getting up and walking out of his room, John resorted to his old habits, when unsure about a situation, walk around and just kind of chew on what it is that you heard, saw, whatever. So that is what he did.

He went down the hallway back toward the Chimera Room. There was still quite a bit of commotion in there as people were lingering and chatting away. Sitting around and having that 2nd and 3rd cup of coffee while picking at the cake that sat in front of them.

John lingered in the hallway and observed. He thought to himself on why a group of doctors would want to convince people that there was no God. Why would they want to do this by means of creating a new race of people?

John strolled into the Chimera Room and walked the perimeter which was mostly comprised of ceiling to floor windows. He walked as he looked out into the courtyard. The impossibly blue sky and the lush, green grass growing and the constant yet low humming sound of people talking, birds chirping and some other sound that was not distinct enough for him to make out.

John walked around the courtyard and sat down on a stone retaining wall that ran the length of the sidewalk that he was walking on. He sat and stared silently at the ALPS building. People walked in and out of the building. Most had an empty look on their face and seemed to be thoughtless in their activities. They looked to him as being programed to repeat the same thing repeatedly; like on a loop. The more he stared at them, the more he grew curious on their behavior. He noticed, an oddity that he had not noticed before, no one was talking to each other. His eyes scanned the entire courtyard to see if this same anomaly was consistent or if he just happened to notice something that, yes was unusual, but isolated. Sure enough, there were no social interactions. Everyone was walking in and out of the building, up and down the sidewalk, across the courtyard and sitting at numerous picnic tables. That was exceptionally odd because the people that were sitting at the picnic tables, they were literally just sitting there; they were not doing anything nor talking to anyone; just sitting.

John thought back to what he had overheard in the room at the end of the hallway and started to assign logic to what he was seeing versus what he had heard.

There would be two races of people: one reanimated and seemingly perfected and one disease ridden with a predisposition for death due to their genetic weaknesses. Logically, a perfected race would be cleansed from any type of genetic shortcomings. They would not be susceptible to addiction; they would not be susceptible to viral or bacterial infection. These individuals would have a normal white blood cell and red blood cell count. Their glucose would be regular and lipid count would be regular. Their weight would be aligned with body structure and most importantly, they would be conditioned to think a certain way. They would be conditioned to believe social interaction should happen only for purpose. This needed purpose would eliminate the existence of coveting what each other have as they would be conditioned to think that they were chosen to be reanimated into The Therab Race and therefor are perfect as they are intended to be.

As John rationalized what he had heard, he looked around more but this time, noticing even more details that he had not before. There was visible balance of men to women; broad pallet of skin tones; ranging from the darkest to the lightest but everyone was, by appearance in perfect health. There was not a single person overweight. Everyone looked vibrant, energetic and healthy. All the men stood at approximately 5 foot 10 inches and all the women stood at approximately 5 foot 7 inches.

John, curious by nature, stood up to preform a small little experiment. He walked up to the ALPS building entrance and approached a woman exiting the building. She was, what he would consider middle of the spectrum in range of skin color; neither pale white nor dark brown. Her hair was what he would consider a dirty blonde that was at shoulder length with a slight bobbed cut to it. If he had to guess her age, he would have guessed between thirty and thirty-five. He smiled to himself when he thought, "Of course, she is Thirty-1; everyone here is Thirty-1". The woman was dressed in a neat, charcoal gray pantsuit. The suit was slim fitted and flattering to her 5 foot 7", slender frame. She looked strong but feminine. She wore modest, black heels and wore a satin, pink button up shirt under her suit coat. John tried to take notice in his observations if her skin was bright and flawless naturally or if it was enhanced with make-up. If he had to guess on the spot, he would suspect that she wore no makeup as the perfected skin tones and texture he would expect to be part the "genetic perfection" he suspected that individuals from the room down the hallway were investigating. John casually approached the woman. He asked the woman in the most casual way that he knew, "Excuse me Miss, I am looking for a pub that I might have a nice cold drink at. Do you have any recommendations?"

The woman looked at John, the mindless gaze she had on her face a moment ago was instantly replaced with shock and an incredulous gasp, "Sir! What are you asking? Why in the world would you think I would know of a place like that! I suggest you go and speak to one of the others if you insist upon going to that type of establishment. But I will tell you this, your kind isn't warmly welcomed here when you show that type of weakness."

"What type of weakness is that?" John inquired. He added to the theatrics with an expression of complete bewilderment.

"The type of weakness that shows a dependency of substance. That dependency is a poison to your body and we," she gestured around, "We do not want that type of weakness bred into or society. I suggest you leave sir."

"Well where am I to go?" John was trying to sound genuinely confused. "I just got here and was told that I am to start a new life and be reunited with my family that has been departed for quite some time."

The woman looked at John with such shock, he thought that at any moment she was going to start screaming. "You mean, you ARE a Therab?"

"Why yes," John answered.

The woman backed up and walked away quickly. She did not turn back, and she did not run to anyone and share what she just experienced. She just simply left.

John really was not at all surprised by her reaction. He recalled leaving his notebook in his room before coming downstairs so instead of writing down his observations, made mental notes of the following: divisive, judgmental and perceived purification.

John waited for the woman to be completely out of site before he started walking the sidewalk in the opposite direction with hopes of finding a person to be an unknowing participant in the second half of his experiment.

In the spirit of true science, John felt it important to somewhat control the variables, so he decided to approach a woman again. This time, he changed his dialogue to satisfy a hunch he was trying to prove out.

John approached a different woman this time. She too was about 5 foot 7" tall. This woman wore a long black A-Line skirt that when to her ankles. It was very form fitted and was accompanied by an off-white turtleneck sweater. The woman wore tall, healed boots that when viewed from behind, could be seen throw the slit of the skirt, went to just below the knees. They had red-brown tone to her hair and piercing green eyes. She wore her hair in a bun that was pinned to the top of her head. She too seemed to have flawless skin and required no enhancements or cover up to hide blemishes, as she appeared to have none. Much like the previous woman, this one too was fit and slender but very feminine in her stature and the way that she carried herself.

"Excuse me Miss," John said approaching the woman. His voice seemed to startle her away from whatever or whomever her attention was previously captivated with. "I am new here and was told that there is a library somewhere on the campus. Can you please lend me some guidance?"

"We have several libraries here," the woman immediately answered with a warmth in the tone that John did not at all detect in the other woman. Ironically enough, John would have expected the warmth from the other woman when compared to the piercing gaze of this woman and her green eyes. "What area of study are you inquiring on?"

John immediately responded with a giddy tone that he tried to subdue, "Bio-mechanics and molecular modification, that sort of thing," he replied.

The woman smiled and pointed over John's shoulder saying, "It is just south of the ALPS building in the building marked APEX. Would you like me to escort you over there?"

John shook his head saying, "No thank you Miss, I can find it from here." He turned on his heel and left the woman behind him. He smiled at the irony of the name of the building. The very definition of APEX is to be the highest point of something. A genetically purified world, one that does not believe in God possibly? Science would certainly be a plausible replacement and the research literature reasonably be located here; at the top of this area.

John had no intention of going to the APEX building but rather decided to go and find the only 2 people that he knew, Lorraine and Ray.

Lines have Been Drawn – Volume 9

John casually began to circle back to the ALPS building when he knew he was out of site from the red head. He had no idea what he was going to tell Lorraine and Ray when he found them other than what he had discovered. "What had he discovered though," was what he really wanted to know. He started to catalogue everything that he had gathered up, mentally though until he could get back to his room and back to his notebook. He knew that he had to at least get everything in order chronologically before he tried to explain anything. In a weird way, he almost felt relieved, both emotionally and physically relieved to have something else to redirect his efforts on. The entire study of tissue reanimation was even in his day, a very contentious topic. People who did not understand the science behind it scoffed at the scholars who pursued with a blanket label of them having a God complex. Although he loved his work, it would always lack a certain nobility in his eyes because deep in his heart he wanted to partake in something that would be embraced by the entire human race as being a genuine contribution to humanity; tissue reanimation, no matter how many loved ones would be reunited, would always draw criticism to those who were spiritually devout.

Oh no, this was so much bigger than that. If he was right, and he had a hunch that he was, he was forced into a situation where the main premise was to redefine the human race by genetically controlling the creation of each and every person.

John approached his room and used his palm to enter. The bio-metric reader responded with the door opening. John went to his dresser bureau and collected his notebook and pencil that he had put in there earlier. Turning to the second page, he began to right in bold letters, *"RACE WAR."* He underlined it and wrote *"Sugar."* After that, he wrote, *"Described as being the race of people who have not yet undergone reanimation. They still possess possible dispositions of undesirable traits: addiction, obesity, disease etc. Are revered as being a second class to the Sweetener.*

John then wrote, *"Sweetener."* After it he wrote, *"Genetically modified and selected, uniformly sized and even distribution of flesh tone variations. Free from physical disfigurements and free from any mental and/or emotional frailties. Self-identified elitists who view themselves as being enlightened (?)".* John put a question mark in parentheses as he wrote that. This statement was an unproven hunch that he had however, it was reasonably assumed to be accurate.

John then wrote *"Verified"* and underlined it. Under that he wrote, *"Eliminate the existence of God to diminish Genocide. Deceive the elderly and sick into thinking that they will too be reanimated and die thinking such. Gentrify the new race by genetically modifying them."*

John thought for a moment before writing again. On the next page he wrote *"RESULTS"* and underlined it.

"Division continues between the two new races; conclusion is that humans will always try to find a way to separate each other from one another."

"Why they separate", he wrote. *"Individuals in either race desire individuality along with validation and when that individuality is marginalized or the individual is not validated or is dehumanized, conflict is inevitable."*

"High level conclusion is to not interfere in the process of natural selection."

With that final thought, John inserted his notebook into the breast pocket of his jacket and left his room. He headed straight to The Chimera Room where he had last seen Lorraine and Ray.

As he approached the doorway to the room, soft and unobtrusive ringing let out through the building. For a second, it reminded John of the type of sound that one might here in a department store just before it announced a limited time and supply sale. The ringing was followed up with an announcement that stated, "Attention everyone, for those of you that have completed the orientation and training here at the ALPS facility and wish to pursue progress outside of the campus, please make your way to the monorails located at the south of the campus. They are marked A, B and C. There is no assigned car you should ride in, it will be based solely on capacity and destination. The destinations are as followed, Monorail A will take you to Chicago, Monorail B will take you to Dallas, and Monorail C will take you to New York City. If your monorail is full, please consider a new destination or plan on waiting for the next deployment. Each monorail can carry 20,000 passengers and the travel times vary between 1 ½ hours to 3 hours. Our monorails boast a land speed of 482KM/Hr. and are remotely controlled from our state of the art control center which is ran nonstop by our master engineers. We will begin boarding in 30 min and will depart in exactly 1 hour 45 min. The time is now 12:15PM. Thank you for your time."

The announcement was followed up by another ringing sound which John assumed meant that the announcement had completed. He took out his notebook and based completely off of memory, drew a rudimentary map of the United States. He put a star in the general areas that represented Dallas, New York City and Chicago. All three destinations can be reached between 1 to 3 hours. The speed of the monorail was 482 KM/hr. or 300 miles per hour, he estimated that Dallas and New York City were the furthest and Chicago was the closest. He figured that would put his current location somewhere in the Kentucky or Tennessee areas. He tapped his pencil to his head thoughtfully. John concluded that the likeliness of his current position did make sense. There are still some fairly remote areas in Kentucky and Tennessee where experimental social structures could be developed. He thought for a moment and considered his options; on one hand he could board a monorail (the destination really wasn't relevant) and continue on with this little mystery on his own. On the other hand, he could run like hell and go get Lorraine and Ray, somehow convince them to get on a monorail with him and explain on the way. Being a man of science, he made a quick mental risk assessment. The riskiest part was him having to explain everything to Lorraine and Ray, waste his time doing so because they still do not agree to go with him and he subsequently misses all 3 monorail departures. The downside to that though was that he was well aware that that the probability that he would be thrown into a mix of people whom he wouldn't know and would have no place to go was an absolute certainty. As John was going through these thoughts, he was unaware that he was already walking back towards the ALPS building; that in itself told him that he subconsciously wanted to try to engage both Lorraine and Ray. He knew that if for no other reason than safety, it was best for the 3 of them to stick together.

John hastened his steps back into the ALPS building and made a bee-line back to the Chimera room. He spotted both Lorraine and Ray as they were clearly finishing up their discussion by getting up from the table. Both looked at John in astonishment as he approached. Up to that point, John hadn't demonstrated a huge need to want to interact with them; for the most part, he was very much aloof.

"John," what is it? Lorraine asked.

"You both need to come with me immediately," he answered as he outstretched his arm to usher them toward him.

Intrigued and bewildered, both Lorraine and Ray followed John.

"What's this all about John?" Ray asked with a sense of urgency in his voice. He too was taken back by John's abrupt and unexpected interaction with the two of them.

"I'll tell you about it on the way. Quickly now, tell me, do you prefer Dallas, Chicago or New York?"

"What do you mean prefer?" Lorraine asked?

"Yea, what's this all about?" Ray prodded.

"Just choose, I'll tell you along the way," John insisted.

Lorraine and Ray just looked at each other and shrugged, "Well," Ray began, "This is already weird as hell so I guess Chicago, why not."

Lorraine shrugged in an indifferent sort of way and the three of them briskly walked along side John but with John's clear guidance on where they were going.

"Is this a train station?" Lorraine asked as they approached the monorail substation.

John didn't reply. He simply looked up and followed the signs that pointed 'Monorail A'.

Each car to Monorail A had a car attendant standing outside of it. John approached the first attendant who appeared available and said with a nod, "Sir, we are traveling together and would like to get a car together if possible."

The attendant nodded and ushered the three travelers into the car closing the door behind them.

The car was small, it was approximately 10 feet in length and approximately 5 feet in width. There was a tinted window on both sides length wise and a narrow hatched door on either end; this was presumably to travel in between the rail cars.

The flooring was a clean, gray colored commercial carpeting which would have been uncomfortable to the touch but was excellent at muffling the noise from the movement of the train.

On the far length side of the car were 2 booth benches with a pedestal table rectangular in shape in between them. The table was bolted to the floor and was dark gray to contrast the floor. The booth seats were a lighter shade of gray but not the same shade of the carpet. There were overhead storage compartments above the table which would require the individual to duck down to prevent themselves from hitting their head.

The lighting was a soft LED recessed track lighting system. It was soft but provided ample lighting for the three to sit and discuss things while fully being able to see one another.

"Ok John," Ray began, "What's this all about?"

John hunched over the table and looked at them with such intent that they really couldn't begin to guess what he was about to say. Then he began.

"I was walking around in the ALPS building and came across some sort of meeting that was taking place and what I heard has led me to believe that this," he motioned toward the ALPS complex, "and us, well none of this is what we think it is."

"Ok," Ray said, "What is it?"

"I think it's some type of experimental project being led by some very wealthy but possibly very dangerous people. What I heard them say led me to believe that they are genetically modifying people and reintroducing them into society as some type of 'elite' people. This is being done to create a race war."

"A race war?" Lorraine questioned with obvious suspicion. "And why on Earth would anybody want to start a race war?"

"I'm not entirely sure. Maybe to develop new class system? Maybe to aid in genetic purging? There could be any number of reasons but my hunch is that these 'people'," John used air quotes, "have a specific agenda in mind and nothing about it is for the betterment of any of us."

"So what are you expecting to find in Chicago?" Ray asked.

"Well, I'm not sure exactly but if my hunch is correct, we are going to experience what is intended to happen as soon as we get to Chicago. I don't believe there is anything particularly significant about that location, it's just a destination selected. If my hunch is correct that the ALPS building is located somewhere in Kentucky or Tennessee, we'll have our answer, probably in about an hour or two."

Lorraine looked at John stunned, "I'm sorry, I just don't understand. First, how did you determine how long it would take us to get to Chicago and second, let's go back to what it is that you heard. I'm going to need you to walk us through this a little slower. If you are correct in your time assessment, we should have plenty of time."

John motioned for both Lorraine and Ray to sit down at the benches. Lorraine and Ray sat down next to one another and John sat across from them and pulled out his notebook from his breast pocket. "Ok," he began. "The overall context of the conversation that I had heard earlier was incomplete. I had heard what could arguably be just pieces of a largely woven plan. With that being said, my conclusions are purely conjecture at this point. But that was up until a little while ago before we got on the train."

"Ok," Lorraine nodded. "Let's start with what you pieced together."

John began, "The general over view of what I actually heard is that we are a part of a massive testing project where we are 3 of about 50,000 test subjects. The main objective it would appear, is genetic purification. This purification is being initiated at both a social conditionally level and a genetic modification level."

"What do you mean, purification?" Ray asked.

"Remember when we went through was sort of an orientation? We were told that we are brought back at the age of 31? A seemingly prime age of mental maturity and peak physical strength? And we were referred to as The Therabs? Well, what they are doing is creating a pure race that is free from what would be considered human flaws. Things like disease, addiction, mental illnesses and so on would be purged from this race of people. They would be conditioned to believe that they were selected to be the superior race. It is a sort of synthetic natural selection. Now, I put this to the test before I ran into you two. I approached a woman and told her I was lost and was supposed to go through some kind of change and be reunited with my family. The look of disgust on the woman's face was palpable. She looked revolted. So the social conditioning would appear to be immediate. It's more than an elitist attitude. These people genuinely feel that they are the one's personally hand selected by God to persevere and exist as this purified human. I took some notes," John started to flip through his note book and read out loud. "Sugar, "he started, "Sugar of course represents the natural race. Its contrast of course would be Sweetener."

Lorraine and Ray both looked confused. John stopped and explained, "I used code words. I know it sounds ridiculous but it was the only way that I could keep this all from being jumbled up in my head. I created code words the symbolized what they represented."

Ray and Lorraine glanced at each other before Ray offered up, "It's ok John, it makes sense. Please continue" Ray's tone was soft and almost calming in sound. Seemingly not wanting to upset the apple cart of this crazy old man.

"Thanks," John said. "Listen you guys, just let me get this out and I think it'll make sense. Motive is what you want, these are just the milestones that mark the map on how they get to their final destination and why. Ok, so Sugar versus Sweetener. I suspect the difference are obvious. Synthetic versus natural. Flawed versus Perfect. That sort of thing."

"Ok, let's assume that what you are saying is what the agenda is. Jump the finale of this and explain the motive," Ray stated. His calming tone hardened a little either because he was losing patience or because he didn't think John needed to be treated with "kid gloves" and really wasn't unstable.

"Well," John began, "In my own personal opinion, from what I heard, I think that this is about mind control and some sort of "God Complex" that these people have. These people who are running this charade are literally convincing people that they correct way to exist is the way that they are told they must exist. I mean, let's be clear, this is an environment created for the sole reason of deception. It's isolated and there is nothing to challenge the reality it presents. The people who created this reality get to decide what is acceptable and what is not; whether it be in looks, health or behavior. The world that they've created carves out the narrative that THEY want people to believe. And the big question of why? Well, that's a huge amount of power that wielded by the correct or arguably wrong person or persons, could reshape the evolutionary road of mankind."

"They couldn't keep this up forever though, I mean, someone would eventually figure things out and bust out of the mold right?" Lorraine asked.

"That is what I want to test," John said. "Once we get to Chicago I believe is when my hypothesis will truly be tested."

"What are you expecting to see?" Ray asked

"I think we will see either a bunch of nothing and it'll disprove my entire hypothesis or we will see an inexplicable amount of divisiveness and segregation on scales never seen before in human history and the volatility of the situation will be so enormous that the slightest imbalance would send society into a tailspin of violence and civil unrest. But even if we see the latter. There is one variable so far that I cannot make sense of that's us."

"What do you mean?" Lorraine asked.

"Why are we the outlier that is asking these questions and recognizing that these "social norms", John used air quotes to illustrate the hypocrisy in that statement. "Why isn't anyone else?"

"Maybe we aren't truly Plerabs? Maybe we are still Therabs and this allows us to still have individual thought?" Ray offered up as a potential explanation.

Pointing at Ray, John said, "Yes, good. What else?"

"Well, at orientation they had told us a bunch of stuff about our age being chosen based off of prime strengths and weaknesses of that age, well I don't know about you guys, but all indicators shown, I would say I'm about the 31 year mark so maybe we were partially changed?" Lorraine offered up.

"Interesting," John said. "There are numerous possibilities here and I think that with the little bit of time we have left, we can catalogue what has changed, noticeably changed about ourselves that would support that we are now part of the Plerab Race and then things, such as individual thought," John motioned to Ray as he said this, "As well as other attributes that indicate we are still members of the Therab Race."

"Wow, a Race war," Ray said with a shudder.

"One like we've never seen before," John flatly stated.

"The winner will determine where humanity goes," Lorraine finished with a voice absent of emotion.

"Well, you should be ok Lorraine, you will go to Heaven if you die from this Race war," Ray offered up half laughing and half being serious.

"That's not how it works. Heaven isn't an escape pod for Christians to get the hell out of dodge. The work needs to be done while we are here on Earth." Lorraine curtly stated.

"Oh I'm sorry Lorraine, I didn't mean it like that," Ray sounded genuinely remorseful as he immediately realized that he plunged his whole foot right smack into this mouth by accidently making a mockery or Lorraine's faith. Lorraine offered up a smile that put Ray's mind at ease by letting him know all was forgiven.

The Intercom interrupted their discussion with a brief announcement of "We will be arriving at your destination in approximately 15 min. Please remain seated until the monorail has come to a complete stop, have a nice day."

"Well," John began, "Here we go. Let's stay close and don't make any sudden movements if things look tense. I really have no idea what to expect."

With that, there was a tone that sounded indicating that the monorail was stopped. The Intercom came back on stating, "You've arrived in Chicago, Illinois. You are currently at the Chicago Union Station located on Canal St. The temperature is currently 73 degrees Fahrenheit." There was a click and then silence again.

John mumbled under his breath as the three stood shoulder to shoulder, ""Art is the tree of life. Science is the tree of death."

"Who is that?" Lorraine asked.

"William Blake," John answered.

"I like that," She said.

The doors began opening and what they saw shocked them to the core. There was no going back now.

Advanced Life Process Selection –

Volume 10

A rush of cold air filled the monorail car simultaneously sending a shiver down the spines of Lorraine, Ray and John. They weren't prepared for what they were met with.

Lining up and down the platform was a sea of people. This angry mob lined the rail station and were prepared to greet, in a not so friendly manner, all who vacated the monorail. The mob was screaming holding up signs saying things like, "You're an Abomination" and "You can't play God". Some people didn't say anything but rather displayed themselves as being corpses. They elevated themselves above others and in quite the theatrical way, demonstrated their death by way of noose strangulation or others showed themselves in a Zombie like state with a sign on them reading, "I am no longer a creature of God. I am an abomination. There will be no Salvation for my soul."

Lorraine and Ray were horrified at what they saw but couldn't look away. John had taken out his little notebook from his breast pocket and begin writing vehemently. All three remained in the car while tens of thousands of Plerabs began to offload onto the train platform.

The Plerabs weren't initially aggressive but you could hear the derogatory banter back and forth. One woman yelled out to nobody specifically, "You disgusting deplorable, disease filled maggots!"

Another person yelled out, "They made US in God's image, not you! You're filth! You're nothing! You don't deserve a life; you'll be a burden is all!"

John looked up from his notebook and noticed that the yeller came from a young man, he guessed to be thirty one years in age which he sort of smiled to himself when he realized what he just assessed without even realizing that one of the main premises behind his theory was that the age of thirty one would be the age of all Plerabs.

As more and more people got off the monorail, the noise level increased and ability to hear the distinct commentary was masked and drowned by a barrage of yelling. That in itself John thought to be ironic; all of the yelling made it impossible to hear.

The first sound of glass breaking came from the right of where the three were standing. It was followed up by more shouting and then a loud thud.

"Oh…my…. God," Lorraine stammered. "This is what they wanted?"

"Yes," John said. "I believe it is."

In an instant, the next chain of events happened so quickly that it was impossible to catalogue the chronology of events. The situation went from hostile banter to an all-out war.

Ray didn't say anything. He just stared in disbelief as he saw the lines of people merge into one. These people were tearing each other apart. The strength of their conviction resided solely on the propaganda that they had been told.

A huge thud sound came from their left. Lorraine, reluctantly peered her head out of the train car and looked in horror and disgust. A man had been thrown into the side of the train by another man and 3 more people descended upon the fallen man. His screams at first were muffled by the yelling but then it became clear that they were beating him to death. One person had a metal pole and continuously struck the fallen man in the head until his lifeless body stopped moving.

Lorraine turned her head; she had no desire to see the carnage that remained but knew that it was a ghastly site.

The three spectators slowly backed into the car and grouped together in the furthest corner away from the door.

"What do we do?" Ray asked knowing that there wasn't really a good answer.

"Well," John began, "We can try to wait it out and hope nobody thinks to look in this car. But if they find us, we'll be cornered like rats."

"Why did you even want to come here?" Lorraine pleaded with John.

"I had to know," John said, "What I heard back at the ALPS building needed to be verified."

"Verified? We're probably going to die here because you didn't just trust the science you heard," Lorraine yelled in a whisper.

John smiled in a genuinely warm way, "My dear, I am a scientist. I do not trust the science; I test the science. If we die, then we die but it won't be because I didn't pursue truth."

"Well, I vote for us to try to make a run for it. If we all stick together, and avoid confrontations with anyone, we might be able to get out of this train station and find a place to gain more perspective on what exactly is going on and why," Ray offered up.

"How are you proposing we do this without getting killed?" Lorraine asked.

"Do you believe in God?" Ray asked.

"Of course, I do, you know I do," Lorraine snapped.

"Then we are going to have to have faith that we are exactly where God intends us to be in the exact moment intended. Whatever should happen to us is simply part of God's plan. Isn't that what you would tell me?" Ray challenged.

Lorraine smiled and replied, "Let's go, whatever will be will be."

John didn't have much to contribute to the conversation, he just listened and nodded to Lorraine.

The screams from outside the monorail broke the divine mood which was created for a brief moment. In that brief moment though, all three were shrouded in an inexplicable calmness. Hand in hand, they all stepped off the monorail together.

The grotesque scene was worse than any war pictures they recalled seeing in school. The carnage was reprehensible. Arguably, the way these people were behaving, neither could be glorified in virtuous behavior at all. Their mutual hatred blinded them and recalibrated their moral compass into an oblivion.

The lack of humanity was disgraceful. There was zero respect for life by either side. People were being bludgeoned by one another and enthusiastically dismembered. Lorraine caught a glimpse of a man attacking a woman. At this point, she had no idea which race either belonged to but regardless, the man cornered the woman, tore open her shirt exposing her bare breasts. The man took a long-edged knife and plunged it into the woman's chest. A look of astonishment covered the woman's face as her arms reached out toward the man but only grasped air.

When the man removed the knife from the woman's chest, a stream of blood followed. Without warning, another man approached the knife wielding killer and struck him in the back of the head with a metal pipe. The clubbed man fell to the ground dumbfounded as his attacker relentlessly continued to beat him in the face with the metal pipe. His face quickly turned into a bloody pulp leaving the man an unrecognizable pulp covered corpse.

Lorraine gasped and looked away in horror but she didn't know where to look to as the same violence was surrounding them.

The three continued to walk in a forward direction. They left the monorail behind them and tried to make their way off the platform and away from the train station.

There had to have been thousands of people surrounding them though, making this seemingly easy journey impossible. Every single person seemed to have been detonated like a bomb to go off at the same exact moment. It was complete chaos.

"Keep moving," Ray said. Lorraine could feel the grip of his hand tighten around hers.

"Should we try to help any of these people?" Lorraine asked.

"I would recommend against it," John said. "If you can't tell apart the people, then you have no idea who you are helping and I would argue that not knowing who is who is reason enough to not get involved."

That very moment, a large over bearing man stepped in from the three. He had a menacing look on his face and held a large ax in his right hand. He looked directly at Lorraine and Ray and hissed, "Where are you running off to?"

Ray squeezed Lorraine's hand for a second then shoved her out of the way putting himself in between the large man and Lorraine.

"Listen, we don't want any trouble. We just caught a ride here and that's it. I don't know what this is all about but we're not involved," Ray tried to reason with the man.

"You don't get to choose to not be involved or not, you are on one side
or the other. You are on the side of Plerabs or the side of the Therabs.
There is no middle ground, not anymore. Co-existing doesn't exist."

The large man took a step towards Ray and the long-handled ax on top of
his shoulder, "So which is it? Are you Godly or ungodly?"

"I can't answer that," Ray stammered.

"We are Godly," Lorraine yelled out from behind Ray.

"Then you must fight," the large man bellowed. "You must strike down
the abomination. The soulless and the impure. There is no tolerance
here."

"But this isn't our fight," Lorraine begged.

"One side or the other," the large man repeated. He then took his ax and
swung it at Lorraine's head. The blow came with a loud thud sound and
her face instantly froze in a look of bewilderment. There was an earie
dent in the side of her skull where the butt of the ax hit. At first there was
nothing, then after a pause that seemed unnatural, the skin on her scalp
seemed to come apart and blood began pouring from her head. Her body
collapsed onto its side in a huge heap. There was slight twitching coming
from her body as the last bit of life seemed to be exhausted with every
pulse of blood that left the wound in her head.

Ray gasped in horror. He was speechless and didn't know what to do.
He stood frozen and stared at the large man in disbelief. "What have you
done?" Ray stammered.

"But you who forsake the Lord, who forget my holy mountain, who set a
table for fortune, and who fill cups with mixed wine for destiny, I will
destine you for the sword, and all of you will bow down to the slaughter.
Because I called, but you did not answer; I spoke, but you did not hear.

And you did evil in my sight and chose that in which I did not delight," the large man said as he swung the ax onto his shoulder again. "That's from Isaiah chapter 65, verse 11 and 12. I believe that God sent me here to find you and destroy you. If you aren't going to stop the abomination, then you too must be destroyed. As their ungodliness is running through your veins as well and if you're not stopped, this won't stop." In the next moment, the flash of the ax came down on Ray's head and he too met the same fate as Lorraine.

John had already been backing up away from the large man. He had made his way to the edge of the platform toward an exit. He couldn't truly wrap his head around what he was feeling because it didn't seem to reconcile with what he was seeing. He knew he should be horrified but just wasn't. There was a strange and inexplicable calmness around him and as he grew closer and closer to the exit, the calmness swept over his body more. The large man had shouldered the ax once more as he watched John back up toward the exit. He had a smirk on his face and then in the moment that John reached the door, the man bellowed out, "Woe to the wicked! It will go badly with him, for what he deserves will be done to him!"

John turned and pushed his way through the turn style.

John could see both on the other side of the turn style so he proceeded forward. As soon as he began pushing the heavy metal bars, a white light filled his line of vision and then he saw nothing.

A soft beeping sound filled John's ears after a moment. It became louder and louder the more he solid his bearings were established. After a moment, he fluttered open his eyes and looked around.

He saw what looked like a hospital room and he was laying on what looked like a hospital bed. The room looked very sterile and was bright with white LED lighting.

His vision was blurry but could make out the shapes of people moving around in the room. He could tell who they were but looked to be engaged in their activities and unconcerned about him. They were moving back and forth from machine to machine, checking gages and monitors.

John forced his eyes into focus and sat himself up on his elbows to get a full look at the room. The room itself was fairly large, he estimated that it was about 30 feet by 30 feet. John saw that he was laying down on a gurney and was strapped to it across the ankles and across his mid chest area. He found it interesting that he was strapped at the hands simply because at any moment, if containment was an issue, he could release himself.

"Hello doctor," a woman said while mid-stride in his direction. She wore turquoise-colored scrubs with white colored croc shoes. Her blonde hair was tied back in a loose ponytail, and she had a friendly but young-looking face. "I'm glad to see you are awake, how do you feel?"

"A little bit groggy, more importantly Rebecca, I thought that we had discussed that my arms needed to be immobilized too," John held out his hands to show that they were unsecured.

"They were," she said, "during the time you were out, when we started the process of resuscitating you, I didn't see any need to have you strapped down. I thought that you would be more comfortable being able to move around a bit more freely than what we normally allow," she replied as she began undoing the other straps.

"My dear, none of this is about my comfort, it's about safety. How long was I out this time? About a week? The moment we surpassed more than 5 min of consciousness, is when the straps were employed. A week of my brain being plugged into this synthetic reality could result in a psychological split of some type where my brain no longer and can not distinguish truth from fabrication. The brain responds differently to these synthetic realities, it knows it is not a dream."

John hopped ff the gurney and walked over to the computers and joined three more people in addition to Rebecca.

"So, what whose idea was it to bludgeon Ray and Lorraine?" John asked

"It was mine," a young man with dark brown hair replied. He was sitting at a computer analyzing sequencing language on a monitor. He turned his head to John and removed his glasses. "The bodily response that your body was experiencing was different than the previous times. An increase in heart rate and breathing directly related to interactions you had with them. From the time that the three of you met to the time that the three of you boarded the train. The physiological response was highly indicative of an emotional bond that was forming. If you were forced to watch them get killed, I would expect to see an instant spike in those bodily responses."

"And? Did you?" John asked.

"No," the young man said. "Nothing more than the steady increase I had seen over the last couple of days. That alone could be indicative of a lack of emotional attachment and something else entirely."

"This time was different than before though," John began. He put his hands behind his back and began walking back and forth. "There was a calmness I felt when I was watching Ray and Lorraine get killed. It was as if my fight or flight response never kicked in because on some level, my mind still knew that this whole situation was completely fabricated, and I couldn't provide a true human response to the unrest that was being experienced during extreme activity."

"Well, what about the avatars?" A woman with pointed features and dark hair tightly tied back in a bun ask.

John shook his head, "No, the people representing the Plerabs and Therabs or avatars as you put it, were just responding to algorithms written with the intent to hyperbolize the situation so regardless of anything, the avatars' only purpose was to enflame the situation anyway, nothing about them was a natural situation and must be part of the control group in this situation, they are not part of the variable."

"Honestly," John began, "what I was expecting was a more emotional response when I was overhearing the orchestrators of the entire plot. The creators of the race war and intentional displacement of God. But still, on some level, I wasn't able to get myself there. No, I think we are going to have to change the test environment and subject matter."

All three, Rebecca, the dark-haired man and the pointy faced woman looked at John with their mouths open wide. "Are you saying to Go Live?" Rebecca asked. "We can't it's never been done before and it could be disastrous."

"Do you want true data points or not?" John asked. "Remember what you signed up for. Science doesn't have a moral compass. Truth is neither right nor wrong, remember that my dear. And we are after truth. We are after the truth of influence and redefining reality and the emotional impact it could have on an individual. What's our motivating driver? Artificial intelligence and the utilization of it to create a civil and equitable world for all. A utopia if you will."

"Wayne," John turned his attention to the dark-haired man, "We'll need to draft out summary of this week's findings with an expectation of next steps. I want to have this submitted to the board tomorrow so please start taking notes."

"Now?" Wayne asked. "You were just now getting out of the AI environment."

"Now young man," John said as he smiled off toward something that it seemed only he saw, "Now is all that we have. Now, then, let's begin."

John cleared his throat and began dictating to Wayne, "The day is Friday, January 10, 2020. My name is Doctor John Anderson. This is project AI2020 – BNE. The scope of this project is to study and understand behavior and neural response to artificial intelligence stimulus. This project began in 2018 where live interaction insertion was facilitated, and increments of insertion were progressively lengthier and lengthier. On January 3, 2020, the longest duration of the live interaction of the project was exactly one week and ended on January 10, 2020. This summary is the findings. After such summary, a recommendation on how to proceed will be provided.

The preparation up the live interaction of the project was to develop an environment where an individual was integrated into an artificial intelligence situation. The controlled mechanisms were the following: three subjects where only 1 was an existing person and the other 2 were avatars. The two avatars were pre-programmed to be skeptical of subject

1 and would subsequently build a bond with one another and would acquiesce in the necessary trust of subject 1.

All three subjects would be presented a future situation where they were told that they were in the future and reincarnated to be part of a new race of people. This race of people would then be a genetically superior race with pre-dispositioned negative genes cleansed from their DNA during the reincarnation process.

One of the subjects would be exposed to a conspiratorial plot where the motivation was to create a world devoid of God.

The two remaining avatars would be preprogrammed to have theological discussions and experiences where they would openly discuss with one another to establish a narrative of innate and undisputable faith and belief.

In the last week of the experiment, subject 1 would demonstrate physiological responses which ordinarily would be associated to emotional responses to variable stimulus. In order to hyperbolize those responses, subject 1 would be placed in an environment created to encourage civil unrest and violence. Subject 1 would be forced to watch the murders of the avatars known as subject 2 and subject 3. With such extreme surroundings, an expectation of fight or flight was expected to the response to the AI creating and promoting such undesirable surroundings. Regrettably, subject 1's fight or flight mechanisms were never fully activated is the speculation is that subject 1's brain was able to bypass the situation created by the AI and remain aware that the situation was in fact fabricated. I know this to be certain as it was myself who was subject 1.

The second phase of this experiment will require expansion of the test environment and will require real live test subjects. We will want to use the AI as the control mechanism in this experiment and apply it to live subjects who are completely unaware of the test itself. We will need to use a communication mechanism to get specific messages out there. Social media platforms would be a good resource as they too could in fact be controlled using the AI. That leaves our only variable being the test subjects. The control groups will be simple, those on social media and those not on social media. We will require a substantial amount of data mining to generate the databases of these test subjects. I will require shopping records, phone records, geo tracking etc. from both groups. We will monitor and log all of these happenings. We will need to incorporate some type of bio-metrics or tracking mechanism that can be stored in a data repository that can be later analyzed."

"Doctor," Wayne asked when he finally stopped writing."

John looked up.

"Doctor what really is the purpose for all this?"

John smiled and said, "Mankind is a wonderful entity but can be very self-destructive. I don't want to control mankind, I don't think anyone has that right, but what if, for lack of better terms we say the scope is to influence mankind. Influence mankind to do the right thing and we are just giving them a little nudge."

John sighed and removed his glasses. He began wiping the lenses and said, "What is the most effective and efficient tool to track 6 billion people though. This is a huge subject base."

"Doctor," Rebecca said, "I think you better look at this."

John walked over to Rebecca and followed her gaze to a television that was televising a news reporter. On the bottom of the screen was a ticker that seemed to be giving population numbers of different countries. The ticker looped back to the beginning eventually and a headline read "Total reported infections" and began cycling through the countries again. Now paying more attention, John listened to the woman speak, "Now I would like to provide you with the most current information we have. Please know that we are still early in this response and the situation is still evolving hour by hour and day by day. On December 30th, Delhi reported an outbreak of respiratory disease coming out of Mumbai India. Mumbai, about 768 miles south of Delhi is home to world's largest film industry, Bollywood with a population of more than 19 million people. Now it's not said to have originated in either Delhi or Mumbai but rather linked to another respiratory situation happening elsewhere."

John muted the television and walked away from the television toward his office smiling ear to ear.

"John," Rebecca asked, "What is it?"

"I have an idea," John replied with and nothing more.

www.ingramcontent.com/pod-product-compliance
Lightning Source LLC
Chambersburg PA
CBHW071909120726
48001CB00005B/1667